"Cash, is something wrong?"

He looked at her for a long moment before finally answering. "Other than my realizing how badly I treated you?"

"Yes."

"I'm just realizing how many wrong turns I've taken since I left Forever."

He was lying to her.

And then he abruptly changed the subject by looking at her, a hint of a smile curving his mouth. "A deputy, huh?"

"Why not? I was always interested in criminology," she reminded him.

"I know, but I guess I thought that you were ultimately going to go into ranching. That criminology was, you know, like a hobby with you."

"I guess that maybe you didn't know me as well as you thought."

"No," he agreed sadly. "I guess not."

To hell with backing off.

And she intended to fix whatever was wrong with Cash. For old times' sake.

Dear Reader,

Welcome back to Forever, the little Texas town you first encountered when Sheriff Rick Santiago discovered a baby on his doorstep. A lot has happened to the peace-loving citizens since then, and it's his deputy Alma Rodriguez's turn to have her story told.

Ten years ago Alma was in love with Cash Taylor, who went off to college on the west coast to make something of himself so that they could begin their future. However, along the way he was at first seduced by big-city life, and then lost his soul there. He felt he was no longer worthy of someone like Alma, who was feisty, loyal and loving. But when his grandfather, the man who raised him after his own parents died, asks him to be his best man at his wedding, Cash cannot bring himself to say no. When he arrives, Alma is determined to keep a tight rein on her heart, and Cash is just as determined not to open his heart again because the consequences would be just too great. Ah, the best laid plans of mice and men (and women)…

As always, I thank you for taking the time to read my book, and from the bottom of my heart, I wish you someone to love who loves you back.

Best,

Marie Ferrarella

Lassoing the Deputy

MARIE FERRARELLA

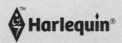

TORONTO NEW YORK LONDON
AMSTERDAM PARIS SYDNEY HAMBURG
STOCKHOLM ATHENS TOKYO MILAN MADRID
PRAGUE WARSAW BUDAPEST AUCKLAND

Recycling programs
for this product may
not exist in your area.

ISBN-13: 978-0-373-75406-9

LASSOING THE DEPUTY

Copyright © 2012 by Marie Rydzynski-Ferrarella

All rights reserved. Except for use in any review, the reproduction or
utilization of this work in whole or in part in any form by any electronic,
mechanical or other means, now known or hereafter invented, including
xerography, photocopying and recording, or in any information storage
or retrieval system, is forbidden without the written permission of the
publisher, Harlequin Enterprises Limited, 225 Duncan Mill Road,
Don Mills, Ontario M3B 3K9, Canada.

This is a work of fiction. Names, characters, places and incidents are
either the product of the author's imagination or are used fictitiously,
and any resemblance to actual persons, living or dead, business
establishments, events or locales is entirely coincidental.

This edition published by arrangement with Harlequin Books S.A.

For questions and comments about the quality of this book
please contact us at Customer_eCare@Harlequin.ca

® and TM are trademarks of the publisher. Trademarks indicated with
® are registered in the United States Patent and Trademark Office, the
Canadian Trade Marks Office and in other countries.

www.Harlequin.com

Printed in U.S.A.

ABOUT THE AUTHOR

Marie Ferrarella is a *USA TODAY* bestselling and RITA® Award-winning author who has written over two hundred books for Silhouette and Harlequin Books, some under the name of Marie Nicole. Her romances are beloved by fans worldwide. Visit her website at www.marieferrarella.com.

Books by Marie Ferrarella

To
Helen Conrad
Who Has Gone
To A Galaxy
Even Further Away
Than Before.
Miss You.

Prologue

He almost hadn't seen it.

The letter had arrived in his mailbox early this afternoon, tucked in between meaningless advertisements, flyers and catalogs offering him everything from overpriced steaks, uniquely packed and shipped overnight to his Beverly Hills apartment, to useless toys and gadgets only "the discerning professional could appreciate"—or hope to pay for, for that matter.

He'd tossed the lot of them into the garbage, but his aim was off and several pieces of mail fell to the kitchen floor instead of into the silver garbage pail.

He stooped to pick up the fallen pieces in order to throw them away, and that was when he found his grandfather's letter stuck in between the catalogs.

Even so, he almost hadn't opened the envelope.

He loved the man dearly. Harry Taylor was his only living relative and the best person—man or woman—that he knew, but the ever-widening dark vortex where he had resided these past four months was growing too large for him to crawl out of anymore.

He wanted his pain, his guilt to finally be over.

Others might have forgiven him for what had happened, but he couldn't forgive himself, and lately, the burden had gotten to be too much for him to handle.

But the letter continued to call to him.

His grandfather, who staunchly refused to have anything to do with "modern nonsense" like computers or the internet, preferred to communicate the old-fashioned way and had written the letter using pen and paper.

Holding the envelope in his hand, Cash Taylor smiled for the first time in weeks, thinking fondly of the man who had written this.

His grandfather had always been there for him, taking him and his mother in when his father was killed in a freak accident on an offshore oil rig. And the man became his sole guardian when his mother died less than a year later, losing her battle with cancer.

A simple, hardworking, decent man, his grandfather knew nothing about what had happened, what was going on presently in his life.

His days on the ranch and living in Forever represented the best years of his life, Cash recalled, not for the first time.

Very slowly, he opened the letter. It wasn't a long missive, as his grandfather had never been enamored with his own words. Consequently, the letter was incredibly short.

I'm getting hitched again, boy. To Miss Joan! Can you believe it? I finally wore her down. Wed-

ding's on a Saturday in three weeks. I know you're real busy, but it would really make me proud to have you there, standing up for me. I miss you, boy.
Grandpa

That was all.

Folding the letter again, Cash tucked it back into the envelope. There was an ache in his soul, a yearning for what had once been.

"I miss you, too, Grandpa," he whispered. "More than you could possibly know."

In all the years that he had lived with the man, his grandfather had never come right out and asked him for a favor. But this invitation was clearly a request for a favor—his presence at the ceremony.

Cash looked at the gun he'd purchased just this week. The gun he'd bought to put him out of his misery.

The same gun, it now occurred to him, that would put his grandfather *into* misery.

He couldn't pay the old man back for everything he'd done, for all his kindness, love and patience by killing himself. It wouldn't be right *or* fair.

Cash picked up the weapon and crossed to his lavish bedroom with its vaulted ceiling and marble-tiled fireplace. He slipped the gun into the back of the bottom drawer of his bureau.

Disappointing his grandfather was not an option.

He was going to the wedding. There was time enough when he got back to do what he felt he had to do.

It wasn't until later that he realized the invitation was a lifeline he'd grabbed on to and held with both hands. His grandfather had saved him for a second time.

Chapter One

Sheriff Rick Santiago paused on his way back from the coffee machine, a filled mug in his hand. He looked thoughtfully at one-third of his team, his only female deputy, Alma Rodriguez. There was an odd expression on her face and she appeared to be at least a million miles away.

She'd been like that since yesterday and it just wasn't her usual, cheerful behavior. He was accustomed to the raven-haired woman smiling and humming to herself.

He wasn't used to seeing sadness in her brown eyes. "You doing okay, Alma?" he asked, his voice low and confidential.

Surprised at being addressed, Alma dragged her mind back to the sheriff's office and tried her best to focus on her boss's voice. It wasn't easy when her mind was going off in three different directions at once. "Sure. I'm fine. Why?"

"I don't know, you look a little…off," he finally said for lack of a better word to describe what he'd been witnessing these past two days.

"No, I'm fine," she answered with perhaps a tad too

much enthusiasm. "But thanks for asking," she added, hoping that would send Rick back to his broom closet of an office and thus bring an end to further questions.

Ordinarily, she would have loved nothing better than to lean back and talk with the sheriff, a man she not only admired, but liked. Forever being the semi-sleepy little Texas town that it was, there wasn't all that much to do when the town's two alcohol devotees weren't staggering down the street because they'd imbibed just a wee bit too much, or Mrs. Allen's cat didn't once more need coaxing out of the tall front-yard tree.

And as for Miss Elizabeth, she hadn't wandered down Main Street in her nightgown in nearly a year.

Crime, such as it was in Forever, was definitely down, allowing her to have too much time on her hands. And consequently, too much time to think about things she didn't want to think about.

Like Cash Tyler's return, however brief.

She wasn't ready for it.

Harry Monroe had dropped his bombshell on her yesterday, gleefully telling her his grandson, Cash, was coming for the wedding.

Her stomach had been pinched in half ever since.

"Reason I'm asking," Rick went on, leaning his hip against the side of her desk for a moment, "is because, besides that look of preoccupation on your face, the coffee you made this morning is just this side of lethal." He paused to take a sip of the hot, inky brew, as if to show her that he had managed to survive the drink. "Now, I don't mind it that way, and most likely Joe won't, either," he said, referring to his deputy brother-in-law, Joe Lone Wolf. "We like our coffee almost solid. But Larry, well, Larry just might threaten to sue you." Humor curved his mouth as he referred to his third deputy, Larry Conroy, who was not the most mild-mannered man under *any* circumstances. "After he gets up off the floor and stops sputtering and choking, of course."

It wasn't that Larry was delicate exactly, but the man was downright picky about everything. While nothing ever pleased the man, this would definitely set him off on a marathon complaining session, he thought.

"My thinking is that maybe you put in twice as much coffee this time around," he pointed out kindly, as if her error was the most natural one in the world. "Knowing how meticulous you normally are, I'm thinking that maybe you've got something on your mind."

Rick leveled his dark eyes at her, giving her a look that had been known to make ten-year-old candy thieves confess to their crimes in an instant. It'd worked pretty well on the few suspects he *had* had to interrogate. Then he got down to what he really wanted to say to his deputy. "Something you'd like to get off your chest, but don't really feel comfortable talking about at home?"

Alma's family was comprised of five brothers and her father. It had been that way for a while now and her home life wasn't really geared toward anything feminine. Normally, that was fine with her, since, for the most part, she'd always been a tomboy. Competitive to a fault, she took great pleasure in beating her brothers at whatever challenge came their way. But there were times, she had to admit, when she longed for another woman to talk to, to confide in. Granted, those times were few and far between, but they did occur.

Like these past couple of days.

Rick had noticed that, for the past two days, his energetic deputy looked anything but. He'd noticed a change, a difference in her demeanor. Her body was here, but her mind was somewhere else. He figured that as her boss—and as someone who cared—he wanted to know exactly where that was.

"What I'm saying," Rick continued when she didn't say anything, "is that you can talk to me. Anytime," he stressed. "In or out of the office."

A small smile curved the corners of her mouth. "I know that and I appreciate it." She did her best to look as if she was brightening up. "But there's nothing wrong, really."

He knew resistance when he saw it, so for now he didn't push the matter. "Except for the coffee," he pointed out, raising his semi-filled mug.

"Except for the coffee," she echoed in agreement. "Sorry about that." Pushing her chair away from her desk, Alma rose to her feet. "I'll go water it down before Larry has a chance to drink it."

"Good idea." Rick turned away and headed toward his office. To the best of his recollection, it was the first time that Alma had ever lied to him. But he wasn't about to push her. She'd come around in her own time and he intended to be there for her when she did.

It occurred to him, as he sat down at his desk and looked at the framed photograph of his wife and infant daughter, that Alma might feel better talking to Olivia. Sometimes women opened up to other women.

As he took another sip of the leaden coffee, the sheriff thought about sending his wife to Alma on some pretext and then suggesting that the two of them go out for lunch. Maybe his deputy would feel more inclined to talk outside the office. Something was bothering her and he sure as hell intended to get to the bottom of it one way or another. He didn't like seeing his people troubled.

Alma emptied out the nearly full pot of coffee into the sink in the tiny kitchenette. As she looked at the black mass that she had prepared earlier going down the drain, she had to admit that the coffee could have easily passed for mud. She was surprised that the sheriff was actually drinking it.

She made certain she didn't let her mind wander as she prepared another pot.

That was stupid of her, Alma upbraided herself. To get so lost in her own thoughts that she hadn't paid attention. That just wasn't like her. She was the one who could always multitask, juggling three or four things at once.

The sheriff had been right, she thought ruefully, measuring out exact amounts of coffee. She'd added twice the amount of coffee per cup when she'd made

the coffee this morning. That was completely unaccept-
able, not because she had made a terrible pot of coffee,
but because she'd allowed her mind to wander to that
extent.

Okay, so she didn't have to be constantly on her toes
the way her counterparts in the major cities had to be.
Here, there were no life-and-death scenarios—outside
of fire season, she qualified. But that was no excuse.
She was letting Cash mess with her mind and he wasn't
even here yet. What was she going to be like when he
was?

You'll be fine, you hear me? Fine, she told herself
fiercely.

It might not actually be fire season yet, she amended,
but it sure felt like it to her. Except this was a different
kind of fire. It was fire of the heart, she thought with
a pang as she mentally counted the number of cups of
water she was pouring in. God forbid she wound up
doing something else wrong and sending everyone in
the office running over to the walk-in clinic run by Dr.
Davenport, complaining of stomach cramps.

*You've got to get a grip, Alma. He's only a man.
Cash Taylor is probably fat and married and nothing
like you remember. So snap out of it!* she ordered herself.

She just couldn't get his face out of her mind. His
face the way he'd looked that last time they had been together. Right before he left Forever. And her. For good.

"You okay, Alma?"

This time it was Joe Lone Wolf asking. He was

standing right next to her, she realized with a start. She hadn't heard him come up, but then the man was a Navajo and he had a tendency to make as much noise as a shadow when he walked.

"Yes," she bit off, "I'm fine. Why are you asking?" she demanded.

Joe took a step back, as if her temper had a physical side to it and it had pushed him away from her.

"Well, for one thing, you're frowning," he told her. "I don't think I've ever seen you frown before. From the inside," he emphasized. "It made me think that maybe something was wrong and that I could help." He nodded at the pot. "Is it ready yet?"

"Another couple of minutes," she replied, relieved to have the subject changed.

She had to stop being so defensive. Rick and Joe were only showing concern. They cared about her.

Unlike Cash.

She did her best to smile. "Nothing's wrong," she lied. That made two, she thought, wondering what her limit for lies was.

Two?

Ten?

Two hundred? Just where did she draw the line? It would have been so much better if she just didn't care. But she did. "I'm just thinking about what I was going to bring to the wedding as a gift for Miss Joan."

"Hey, don't want to leave Harry out," Larry, overhearing her, chimed in as he came into the kitchenette. "They're going to be a set now, Miss Joan and Harry."

The young deputy shook his head. "Miss Joan, married. Wow. It's going to be really hard picturing her that way." He helped himself to a cup of coffee. "Wonder if that means she's going to raise her rates after they exchange vows."

"What does one thing have to do with the other?" Alma didn't see the connection.

Larry measured out four tablespoons of sugar. Watching him, it was all Joe could do to keep from shivering at the thought of taking in all that sweetness.

"Well, she's going to be starting a new life as a bride, right? That means she's going to want to have a lot of new things, isn't she? New things cost money and her source of income is that diner of hers. Put two and two together, Alma," Larry said loftily. "Miss Joan's going to raise her rates, just you watch." He frowned. "I'm going to have to start bringing sandwiches from home."

"That means you're going to have to learn how to make sandwiches first," Joe quipped quietly.

Larry appeared not to hear, but he heard Alma's protest loud and clear. Miss Joan had a very special place in her heart. The woman had given her a job at the diner when she was fifteen so that she, along with her brothers, could earn money to help their dad with the overwhelming medical costs that were involved in trying to keep their mother alive for just a little longer. Alma knew for a fact that Miss Joan had paid her more than the usual going rate.

"Miss Joan's not going to do any such thing," Alma insisted. "She's not like that. Besides, that's what the bridal shower is for, so that we can give her all those little extras. She's already got anything she might need," she pointed out to the blond deputy. "This is Miss Joan we're talking about. Anything she needs, she's got either at home or at the diner."

"And Harry hasn't exactly been living in a tree all these years," Joe pointed out, joining the discussion and siding with Alma.

Sampling his coffee, Larry found that there was something missing. He put in more cream. His coffee now resembled light tan milk. "True, he's got that ranch of his. And the house," Larry agreed.

The house.

The house where Cash had lived before he'd left for college. Before he'd left her.

The yelp that rose from her lips had been an automatic reaction, happening so quickly she didn't have time to stifle it. The back of her hand had come in contact with the coffeepot. Annoyed with herself, she pressed her lips together as she pulled back her stinging hand.

"Alma, you're going to burn your hand," Larry warned needlessly.

Joe was standing next to her and saw the instant patch of angry red that had popped up. "Hell, she already has," he said. He took her hand, holding on to it by her palm. "C'mon, let's get this under cold water first and then I can make this poultice for you—"

She pulled her hand away from him. The last thing

she wanted was to be fussed over as if she was some helpless damsel in distress.

Get a grip, damn it! she repeated to herself.

"I'm fine, really," she told Joe. Looking up, she saw that Rick had been drawn back to the kitchenette, most likely because she'd just yelped and made a fool of herself. She'd worked hard to make them all respect her and now she was sacrificing it all in a few minutes. This *had* to stop. "All of you, stop hovering over me."

"We'll stop hovering," Rick told her patiently, "when you stop acting as if you're expecting to see the ghost of Christmas past at any moment."

He knew, she thought. Most likely, so did Joe. Damn it, she was supposed to keep her feelings to herself, not have them out in plain sight where everyone could see them on her face.

And feel sorry for her.

"I'm not waiting to see a ghost from Christmas past or from any other event," she retorted. "I'm just a little preoccupied today, that's all. Nothing that none of you haven't been at one time or other—and a lot more than me," she declared.

"Yeah, but you're Alma. You don't do things like that," Joe pointed out in his calm, mild voice. "You're supposed to be the one who keeps the rest of us in line, remember?"

"Flattery, nice way to defuse the situation," Rick commented, amused, after Alma had retreated to the communal restroom to run cold water over the red mark on her hand.

"Works with Mona," Joe said with the barest hint of a smile.

Rick laughed. "Maybe I'll try that on Olivia, see if it works next time she's got her back up about something."

Larry shook his head in disbelief. "Henpecked, both of you."

"Not henpecked," Joe corrected. "Thoughtful."

"And smart," Rick interjected. "You get more flies with honey than you do with vinegar."

"Yeah, if flies are what you're after," Larry cracked.

Joe and Rick exchanged looks. "He's missing the point," Joe commented.

"Completely," Rick agreed. "Get back to us when you're married, Larry. We'll talk."

"Married?" Larry echoed. "You're kidding, right? Same routine every night? No, thanks. I'm never getting married."

"Right. You just keep on living the dream, Larry," Joe said, patting the other man on the shoulder.

"You really don't know what you're missing," Rick told the younger deputy as he walked away.

He meant what he said. Because, for the first time in his life, he knew the difference between just being resigned to his lot and being really happy about it. And Olivia and their daughter made him happier than he had ever thought possible.

Larry muttered something unintelligible under his breath and went back to his desk.

"Jealous," Joe concluded.

"Obviously," Rick agreed. And then he became serious for a moment as they passed the restroom. "Do me a favor. Keep an eye on Alma," he requested in a lower voice, nodding toward the restroom door.

"No problem," Joe said.

On the other side of the door, about to walk out, Alma overheard the sheriff and Joe. There was no point in saying that she didn't need anyone's eye on her. What she needed was for Cash not to come back to Forever and mar what would otherwise be a very festive occasion.

But there was no way around it. Harry had been very excited when he'd told her. Cash was coming back for the wedding and she was just going to have to find a way to live with that until he left again.

It wasn't fair, Alma thought, putting back the coffee can in the cupboard and automatically tidying up the kitchenette. It wasn't fair that she cared after all this time and Cash obviously didn't.

But she'd dealt with everything else that life had thrown at her; she could get through this, as well.

Hadn't she dealt with her mother's illness and with having to pitch in with her brothers to earn extra money to help her father pay all the medical bills that had accrued? Bills that had to be paid despite the fact that in the end, her mother hadn't been saved. She'd succumbed to the insidious disease that had eaten away at her, a shell of the bright-eyed, vibrant woman she'd once been.

And hadn't she dealt with the harsh reality that she

wasn't able to go away to college even as Cash, thanks to his grandfather's insistence, left to pursue his dreams of becoming a lawyer?

She could have just given up then, but she didn't. At that time she'd still believed that Cash would come back to her once he got his degree. Determined that he would never have cause to be ashamed of her, she'd been hell-bent to make something of herself. So, continuing to work at Miss Joan's diner in order to earn a living, she took courses online at night.

It took a while, but she had finally gotten her degree in criminology. She'd always wanted to go into law enforcement and had been overjoyed when Rick had hired her on as a deputy.

Her eventual goal was to become a sheriff if and when Rick decided to move on.

If he didn't, then most likely she would. But all that was for a nebulous "someday." Right now, for the time being, this town where she'd been born was still her home.

A home that was about to be invaded.

She would have to psyche herself up, that was all, Alma silently counseled herself.

After she finished tidying up, she folded the kitchen towel, left it on the minuscule counter and walked back to the main room and her desk.

She was just going to have to–

Her thoughts abruptly came to a screeching halt and then went up in smoke just as her heart went into double time.

Cash was standing, bigger than life, right there in the middle of the sheriff's office.

And right in front of her.

Chapter Two

"Hey, Alma, look who I just found walking by our office," Larry called out. It became apparent that the blond-haired deputy had snagged Cash and brought him in, thinking perhaps that he was doing a good deed. "The city-slicker lawyer is finally paying the country mice back home a visit." Larry chuckled at his own display of wit. It was a given around the office that he was always his own best audience. "How's it going, Cash?" he asked, pumping Cash's hand. "Any of those fancy ladies in Los Angeles manage to lasso you yet?"

"It's going well," Cash replied mechanically. "And no, they haven't." He wasn't looking at Larry when he answered. He was looking at Alma.

And she seemed to be looking into his soul.

That was what he used to say to her, that she was his soul. It was a play on her name, which meant "soul" in Spanish. But, even so, back then, he'd meant it. He'd really felt as if she was his soul. His beginning, his ending.

His everything.

In that last summer, during the space between graduation and his going off to college on the West Coast, no one was more surprised than he was when he found himself falling for her. *Really* falling for her. They had grown up together. When he and his mother had come to live with his grandfather, he'd been seven years old, and after a while, it felt as if he had always lived here and always known the Rodriguez kids.

Hardly a day went by that he and Alma didn't see each other, play with each other. Fight with each other. He was friends with her brothers, especially Eli and Gabe, and she always found a way to tag along, no matter how hard he and her brothers initially tried to ditch her.

It seemed that the more they tried, the harder she was to get rid of. Back then, he'd thought of her as a royal pain in the butt. He couldn't remember exactly when all that had changed, but it had. Slowly, she became his friend, then his confidante, and then, ever so gradually, his *best* friend.

And finally, his first love.

Now that he thought about it, Alma had been part of his every day.

Until he left for college.

He'd left to make a future for himself and for her. That was what he'd told himself, what he'd believed. But somewhere along the line, he'd let himself get caught up with the newness and of life in a major city like Los Angeles. He was the country boy who hailed from a speck on the map and he wanted to be as polished, as sophisticated as the students he saw around him in his classes.

Still, in the beginning, while he was still homesick, he looked forward to Alma's letters. He devoured them like a starving man devoured every last morsel of a meal.

But he soon discovered that his tall, blond good looks and Southern accent attracted more than just a handful of women. Male students befriended him, wanting him to be their wingman, their "chick magnet." And female students just wanted him.

After a while, Cash forgot to answer Alma's letters. And then he forgot to read them. He told himself he was too busy studying for exams, but the truth was that he'd been too busy cramming as much life as he could into his existence. It was as if he'd felt compelled to make up for lost time.

He had still studied hard, but every weekend saw him partying equally hard, each time with a different girl. That way it couldn't be construed as anything serious and the tiny part of him that still had a conscience argued that he wasn't being unfaithful to Alma.

Cash told himself that he was just becoming a more rounded person. He was socializing and making connections that would help his future once he became a lawyer.

Instead, it made him, Cash now realized, as incredibly shallow as the people with whom he socialized.

It had been a hell of a ride, though. Somehow, despite all his frantic partying, he wound up graduating near the top of his class. Offers came in from major law firms to intern with them. He made up his mind quickly. He picked the firm with the highest profile, one that dealt in criminal defense cases.

Once on board, he dedicated himself to becoming the best damn intern Jeffers, Wells, Baumann & Fields had ever had in their one-hundred-and-three-year history. He achieved his goal, rising through the ranks faster than any of the partners who had come before him and were now firmly entrenched in the organization.

And all through his rise, there'd been victories and accolades. And women. Many, many women whose names and faces now seemed to run together.

Somewhere along the line, he didn't know just when, he'd managed to lose his soul without realizing it. It hadn't really bothered him very much.

Until that horrible day when everything just blew apart.

All this went through his head in a nanosecond as he stood, looking at Alma, too hollow to even ache. "So how are you, Alma?" he asked quietly.

It almost didn't sound like Cash. Had she ever known this man? Or had she just imagined it all?

"I'm fine," she answered politely. Then, because the silence felt awkward, she added, "Your grandfather mentioned you were coming, but I didn't expect to see you until just before the wedding."

She didn't tell him that Harry had gone out of his way to tell her—to prepare her—and that she'd dropped the glass she'd been holding, breaking it on the diner's counter when she was given the news.

Cash had initially toyed with the idea of waiting until just before the big day, but he knew that if he waited until then, he might not be able to come at all. By then, the despair that held him captive, that ate away at him daily, might have grown too large for him to handle.

But all this was darkness he wasn't about to share. It was his cross to bear, no one else's.

So instead, he shrugged in response to her words and said, "I had a little extra vacation time coming to me. I thought I might just come early and catch up on things I've let slip away."

Just like that, huh? You come sashaying back and we're all supposed to put on some kind of show for you, is that it?

"Good luck with that," she heard herself saying. With that, she walked past him, deliberately avoiding making contact with his eyes.

His voice followed her. Surrounded her. "My grandfather told me you became a deputy sheriff."

She turned around. Considering that she was wearing the same khaki shirt and pants that the three men in the office had on, it would have been hard to make any other conclusion.

"I did."

He laughed softly, but there was no humor in the sound. "Guess I had to see it for myself."

She glanced down at her uniform, then back at him. "Well, you did."

Even as the words came out of her mouth, Alma almost winced. Could either of them have sounded any more stilted, any more awkward, than they did?

That last summer, before Cash went away to college, leaving promises in his wake, they had talked about everything under the sun and the stars. There wasn't a topic they hadn't touched on.

More than talk, there had been trust. She'd trusted him the way she had never trusted anyone else, not even her brothers. And he had opened up to her, sharing his thoughts, his dreams for a future together with her. When he spoke, he'd created vivid pictures with his words. It had been exciting just to listen to him.

Together, they were going to change the world.

He'd even, at the last minute, she recalled with a pang, urged her to come with him.

But that was one of the impossible dreams.

"I don't have any money saved," she'd protested. Just as it had been with her brothers, every penny she'd earned had gone to help pay off her mother's astronomical medical bills.

It was either that, or stand by and watch her father lose the ranch in order to be able to settle the outstanding account. She couldn't allow that to happen just because she wanted to follow Cash to California.

"The money doesn't matter," Cash had told her with the conviction of the very young. "We'll find a way."

She'd wanted to believe him. Wanted, in the worst way, to go with him.

But her sense of honor, her sense of responsibility,

had prevented her from impetuously leaving everything behind and following Cash. She just couldn't bring herself to turn her back on her father at a time like that, even though she knew that he would urge her to follow her heart and tell her that he understood.

It didn't matter if her father understood. She wouldn't have been able to live with herself.

And so, she'd had to learn how to live without Cash.

The last night they were together, Cash had watched her solemnly and she remembered thinking that she had never seen such sadness in a person's eyes. He'd promised her that he would be back for her.

He'd sworn that he would come back for her.

He'd told her that once he had his law degree and was working for a firm, she could stop working and go to school to get her own degree. He'd told her he would pay for it.

She'd hardly heard him. Her heart was aching so badly at the thought of living a single day without him, she could barely stand it. When she couldn't stop the flow of tears, he'd tried to comfort her. And, as sometimes happens, one thing had led to another.

That was the first time they made love.

He'd left her, with great reluctance, the next morning, promising to be back, to make her proud of him and to love her forever.

Watching him go, his secondhand car growing smaller and smaller against the horizon, Alma had been certain that her heart would break right there and that she would die where she stood.

But she didn't die.

And her heart only *felt* broken.

Somehow, she'd found a way to continue. She wrote him every day. What kept her going in the beginning was waiting for his letters.

The wait grew longer, the letters grew fewer. And shorter. Until they stopped coming altogether.

She remembered that now, remembered how she had felt when she finally made herself admit that he wasn't coming back, not to the town, not to her.

Alma squared her shoulders. "Well, I've got work to do," she told Cash stiffly. "So if you'll excuse me—"

They sounded like two strangers who didn't know how to end an awkward conversation, he thought. And that, too, was his fault.

Just like the Douglas murders were his fault.

"Sure. Sorry," he apologized. "Didn't mean to keep you from anything. Maybe we can get together later," he suggested. If there was a note of hope in his voice, it had slipped out and attached itself to his words without his knowledge or blessings.

Alma's voice was completely flat and without emotion as she echoed the word he'd used. "Maybe."

When pigs fly, she added silently.

"Nice seeing you again, Alma," Cash said by way of parting. "Really nice."

And then he was gone.

Alma didn't even look up.

"Well, that was awkward," Larry announced the moment Cash was no longer in the office.

The last thing she wanted was to have a discussion about this—any of this—with Larry. She was fond of the man, but he had a gift for always saying the wrong thing at the wrong time and she wasn't in the mood to put up with that.

"Larry, I brought brownies in yesterday morning. Why don't you go and stuff them into your mouth?" she suggested, accompanying her words with a spasmodic smile she didn't mean. "They're in the cupboard."

"No, they're not," Larry told her matter-of-factly. There was a touch of sheepishness in his voice when he spoke. Alma eyed him suspiciously and he instantly confessed. "Hey, I was here after hours and I got hungry."

"You ate them all?" she asked incredulously. Why wasn't this man fat? Instead, he was as skinny as a rail. "There were sixteen brownies," she emphasized. She'd brought them in for the others, but then she'd stopped at the diner to see Miss Joan, and Harry had told her about Cash. After that, things were a blur. She'd completely forgotten about the brownies until this moment.

"I know," Larry answered. "I counted them. They were probably the best brownies I ever had. Thanks," he added. He had the good grace to look contrite and embarrassed by his apparent gluttony.

"Larry—" She began to complain that he hadn't left any for the others, but at this point, it was all moot. She just sighed.

"Don't pick on him, Alma," Joe said. He scooted his

chair to Larry's desk for a moment. Reaching over, he patted the other man's stomach. "He's a growing boy."

Annoyed, Larry pushed his own chair back, away from Joe. "Cut it out," he warned.

"All right, kids, knock it off," Rick ordered, deliberately using the word *kids* despite the fact that he was only a couple of years older than any of them.

When he glanced at Alma, there was compassion in his eyes. He'd been raised by his grandmother and he'd protectively looked after his little sister during those years. He was more geared in to the workings of a female mind than the average male and he sympathized with what she was going through.

"You want some time off?" he asked her gently.

That caught her by surprise. "What?" Her eyes narrowed. "Why?"

Crossing over to her desk, Rick turned so that while he faced her, his back was to Larry. He wanted to block the other deputy's view. The office was a fishbowl, but he did what he could to give Alma some privacy.

"I know this is all kind of rough for you," Rick told her.

"It would be," she conceded, then said with feeling, "if I wasn't over him, Sheriff. Really, I'm fine." Rick had always been like another big brother to her. An *understanding* big brother who didn't get off on teasing her the way her real brothers did on occasion. "I appreciate what you're trying to do but it's not necessary. I don't need any kid-glove treatment. I'm the same person I've always been," she assured him. "No need to walk on eggshells or tiptoe around me. Really," she stressed.

"All right. If you want to stay on the job, look into this for me." Taking a piece of paper out of his breast pocket, he placed it on her desk in front of her. "Sally Ronson just called, said that she saw the Winslow boys horsing around in the field beyond the high school. They were smoking." There were two things wrong with that. "They're underage and this is fire season. Get those cigarettes away from them and put the fear of God into them any way you see fit—just remember, we draw the line at flogging."

He said it so seriously that for a second she actually thought that he was.

And then she saw the glimmer of amusement in his eyes. "Got you. No flogging."

Joe, who listened unobtrusively to everything that went on in the sheriff's office, looked up. "The Winslow boys?" Joe repeated, then asked, "Kyle and Ken?"

Rick nodded. "The very same."

Joe shook his head. The two brothers were a rowdy handful.

"Good luck with that," he told Alma. "Those two don't have half a brain between them." And then he raised his eyes to hers. "Want company?" he offered.

She knew what he was thinking. What all of them were probably thinking. That the sixteen-year-old twins were strong young bucks and she would need help getting them to listen to her.

"Thanks, but no," she told Joe. "The day I can't handle two snot-nosed teenage boys is the day I'm handing in my badge."

Rick nodded, relieved that at least some of Alma's fighting spirit was still intact. For a minute back there, when Cash had walked in, he'd had his doubts.

"Go get 'em, Deputy Rodriguez. And if they give you any lip," he said, "bring them back here to me." His eyes met hers. "Understood?"

"Understood," she parroted. And then she smiled. "They won't give me any trouble. Don't go dusting off the jail cell just yet."

After folding the paper the sheriff had given her, Alma tucked it into her back pocket. She did it as a formality. Everyone knew where the high school was and she was more than acquainted with the field he'd referred to. She and her brothers used to hang out there.

As had Cash, she remembered.

Even just thinking of his name made something twist deep in her belly. It would be a hell of a long two weeks.

Walking out, she silently blessed Rick. She was glad to leave the office on a pretext. Rick's initial offer of letting her go home wouldn't have been any good. She didn't want to go home. Being alone with her thoughts right now was worse than being subjected to an afternoon laden with Larry's jokes. She needed to keep busy, but being cooped up in the office with Larry unintentionally saying stupid things wasn't conducive to having a tranquil afternoon, either.

She thought back to Joe's offer to come with her. She actually wouldn't have minded his company, but ever since he'd gotten married, he seemed to be slightly more talkative, slightly more prone to commenting on things. It used to be that he kept mostly to himself and spoke only when he had to. Right now, she would have preferred that version of Joe to the new, improved one. One that didn't feel compelled to offer sympathy or comfort.

All she wanted to do was go on as if Cash Taylor was still on the West Coast. She didn't want to talk about him or think about him.

Not exactly an easy matter, she realized a couple of moments later, given that his image popped up in her mind every second and a half.

That was because she was still in shock, she told herself. And why not? He'd come on like an apparition from her past, walking right into the middle of the sheriff's office. Granted, Larry had propelled him into the room but that still didn't negate the final effect.

Or the fact that her heart had stopped beating and then launched into triple time.

She hadn't thought it was humanly possible for someone as good-looking as Cash to grow better looking over time, especially since she assumed that he had had a sedentary life since he'd left Forever.

But he had.

Those were muscles beneath his custom-made jacket. Firm muscles. They went well with his flat stomach and his taut hips.

As for his face, he seemed to have taken on a more chiseled look. Certainly his cheekbones had become prominent. All in all, it gave his profile a somewhat haunting look.

There was that word again, she thought. *Haunting*. She might as well admit that was the way she felt right now.

Haunted.

Haunted by Cash's memory, by his presence—and by the thoughts of what might have been.

The next couple of weeks were not going to be good. She would just have to resign herself to that and make the best of it.

Easier said than done.

A *lot* easier said than done.

Chapter Three

The area just beyond the back of the high school couldn't actually be called a park. It was a clearing with several sun-bleached benches scattered about and a lot of grass in between. Summer evenings invited couples seeking a private moment or two. During the day, children occasionally still brought their imaginations and played timeless games that didn't require electricity.

Today the clearing was empty. Except for the Winslow twins, as had been reported. And, also as had been reported, they were both smoking. Each had staked out a bench and was sprawled out, sending smoke rings up into the hot wind.

Parking her Jeep close to the clearing, Alma got out and crossed over to where the twins were sitting. Her eyes swept over them and she nodded.

"'Morning, boys."

Startled, one of the twins—Ken, the slightly shorter one—sat up straight. "'Morning, Miss Alma," he responded somewhat nervously.

His twin, Kyle, said nothing. He merely glanced in her direction and nodded. Kyle had always behaved as if he thought himself to be the cooler one of the two. She'd come to favor Ken herself.

When she regarded the latter, he appeared not to know what to do with his cigarette.

Alma kept her voice friendly but firm. Her best asset when dealing with teenagers was that she could vividly remember what it was like to be that age. And how she had felt being chided by an adult. It helped temper her words.

"Put them out, boys," she told the twins. "You know you're too young to be smoking cigarettes, even if they were good for you, which they're not."

In defiance, Kyle took another long drag from his cigarette, then slowly blew out the smoke. As it swirled away from him, he smirked as he slanted another look at her.

"You gonna tell us that smoking cigarettes is going to stunt our growth?" The suggestion made him laugh. At sixteen, both twins were close to six foot six, like their father and older brother.

"No," she said, walking up to Kyle and physically removing the cigarette from his hand, "I'm going to tell you that smoking cigarettes at sixteen is against the law." She snubbed out the cigarette against the back of the bench.

Out of the corner of her eye, she saw that Ken was about to throw his own cigarette on the ground and step on it to extinguish it. He wasn't being perverse, like his brother, she realized. He just wasn't thinking.

She relieved Ken of his cigarette, too, and put it out

the same way. "And besides, it's fire season," she reminded the brothers. "You have to be extra careful that a stray spark doesn't hit something flammable."

Satisfied that both cigarettes were out, Alma looked at the two offenders. Most likely, this had been Kyle's idea. He was the persuasive one of the pair. Ken would always follow him, afraid not to.

"Okay, I don't want to see you smoking for another two years and, if you're smart," she added, looking at them pointedly, "never."

Kyle bristled. He'd never liked being reined in. "Ain't you got anything more important to do than to come by and make us put out our cigarettes?"

"Not at the moment," she answered honestly.

Ken looked at her sheepishly. "You gonna tell our old man?"

Dan Winslow was known to be strict with his sons and there were no second chances. First offenses were dealt with quickly and harshly.

Alma saw no point in involving the man if she could get his sons to stop.

"Not this time," she told Ken, breaking the cigarettes in half and then dropping them into the trash after she checked to make sure that the unlit ends were no longer warm. "But if I catch you at it again, then yes, I will. And he's your father—call him that. Not 'old man.' He deserves your respect."

Kyle laughed shortly. "You've never seen him getting out of bed in the morning."

"No, I have not," she readily agreed. "But just remember, we're all going to get there someday including you—and that's if we're lucky." She could tell that Kyle was eager to see her leave. *I'm not stupid, boy.* "Oh, and one more thing," she said in her most innocent voice, "I'll take that pack of cigarettes you have in your pocket, Kyle."

She saw Ken flush. Kyle moved back, as if distance could prevent her from taking the pack. "It's not ours," he protested.

Good. At least she wouldn't have to lecture the grocery store owner about carding his underage customers when they tried to buy cigarettes. "Oh? Then whose is it?"

"The pack belongs to our dad," Ken blurted out even as his brother gave him a dirty look.

That means you're going to get busted, she thought. She remained standing where she was, holding her hand out and waiting.

"If he misses them, tell him he can come by the sheriff's office and get them anytime." With pronounced reluctance, Kyle dug into his shirt pocket and surrendered the pack of cigarettes to her. She nodded and smiled. "Have a nice day, boys. And remember, keep your lungs clean."

Alma got into her vehicle and drove away. In the rearview mirror, she could see the twins arguing with each other. Probably trying to decide what to tell their father when he questioned them about the missing pack of cigarettes.

Alma smiled to herself.

Having resolved the situation to her satisfaction for the time being, Alma was about to head back to the sheriff's office, then changed her mind. It wasn't lunchtime yet, but it was close enough to noon for her to take an early lunch. She decided that for once, she'd give in to herself.

Besides, she needed the sight of a friendly face.

The thought of stopping by the diner and seeing Miss Joan appealed to her.

The diner was like a second home to her, after the great many hours waitressing there. Granted, she wasn't very hungry—seeing Cash had tied her stomach into a knot and killed whatever appetite she might have had— but she could do with the company. Female company.

She loved her father and brothers dearly and had done her best to keep up with the lot of them. For the most part, she'd succeeded and if they suddenly weren't around, she would miss them more than words could say.

That being said, there were times when she found it nice just to let her guard down. Just to be a softer version of herself without having to prove anything to anyone—or feel as if she had to.

That involved talking to a woman. An understanding woman. And Miss Joan, despite the crusty exterior she liked to project, fit the bill to a T.

As usual, Miss Joan was behind the counter when she walked in. The woman looked up the moment she opened the door. One glance at her unlined face— remarkable considering her age—and Alma knew that

Miss Joan knew exactly what she was going through. And why she was here at this hour.

"C'mon in, girl. Take a load off," Miss Joan called out, beckoning her over to the counter. She glanced around and instructed the waitress closest to her, "Julie, go get Alma here a tall, frosty glass of lemonade, please."

Lemonade sounded perfect. Trust Miss Joan to know just what to offer. Alma slid onto the seat at the counter. All she wanted to do was sit here quietly and listen to Miss Joan talk. About anything. There was something comforting about the woman's cadence, as if just hearing her talk made everything better.

"That's all right, Miss Joan," Alma began. "You don't have to go to any trouble on my account. I just want to sit here and—"

She got no further in her protest, but then, that was a given with Miss Joan. The woman overruled everyone, God included, Harry liked to say.

"It's on the house, honey," Miss Joan interjected. One hand fisted at her hip, she pretended to level a sharp look at Alma. "You're not going to insult the bride-to-be two weeks before her wedding by turning down her offer, are you?"

Alma smiled. As if anyone could say no to the woman. "Wouldn't dream of it," she said with a smile. "Thank you."

Julie came and placed the tall lemonade in front of her and retreated. Miss Joan waited until the waitress left, then leaned in over the counter and, in a low voice, asked, "So you saw him, didn't you?"

There went her stomach again, Alma thought, annoyed with herself. It tightened so hard she found it difficult to breathe. Still, she feigned ignorance. "You mean Cash?" she asked innocently.

Miss Joan gave her a look that said she had no time for nonsense. "Don't play coy with me, girl. Of course I mean Cash." And then she laughed shortly. "Really doesn't sound like much of a name for a grown man. Especially not for a lawyer."

Alma recalled that Cash had once told her that when he reached his goal and finally became a lawyer, he was going to use only the initials of his first and middle names on his letterhead. His unfortunate first name arose from the fact that although his father was rushing to get his mother to the hospital on time, nature was against him and he didn't make it. His mother wound up giving birth to him in the backseat. To distract her, his father had had the radio on. Johnny Cash was singing when the infant drew his first breath.

Since they'd been hoping for a girl and had no boys' names picked out, his mother named him after the country-and-Western icon. Cash used to say that he was extremely grateful that Loretta Lynn hadn't been singing at the time.

"Yes, I saw him," Alma said quietly.

Miss Joan nodded. "Did you two talk?"

Alma held the lemonade glass with both hands, focusing on nothing else for the moment. She took a long sip through the straw, then shrugged as if talking to Cash or not talking to him was all really one and the same to her.

"A few words," she acknowledged, knowing Miss Joan wasn't going to let this go until she said *something*.

"So, you didn't talk," the woman concluded knowingly.

No, not really, Alma thought. Out loud she said, "There's nothing to talk about anymore."

The hazel eyes seemed to bore right into her. Alma felt like squirming, but she managed to stay perfectly still under the scrutiny.

"Since when have you taken up lying?" Miss Joan asked.

"I'm not lying," Alma insisted. A little of her temper emerged. "What we had was a summer romance and then he went off to college and I didn't." Again she shrugged, doing her best to act as if she didn't care about Cash or about what had happened that long-ago summer. "Not much of a story, really."

"That's because you left a lot out," Miss Joan pointed out sternly. "Like the fact that Cash broke your heart."

That was giving Cash too much power over her, putting too much importance on the time they had spent together. Alma lifted her chin defiantly.

"We were very young," she insisted. "We had no business falling in love."

"And yet you did," Miss Joan concluded simply. "You're not going to have any peace until you have it out with him and find out why he didn't come back."

There was no need to ask him that. "I *know* why he didn't come back, Miss Joan. It's simple. He liked that life better." *Better than me.* "And talking about it from now until the cows come home isn't going to change anything."

"Might be a change for the cows," Miss Joan quipped. She was feeling Alma's frustration and sympathizing with it. "But what it also might do is open the door to changes in the future. Hey, you're never too old to have things happen." This time Miss Joan's eyes were shining. "Look at me."

"Hey, how about me? I love looking at you," Harry said in his booming voice as he walked into the diner just in time to overhear the last line.

Walking up to the counter, the silver-haired man leaned over and gave his intended bride a quick kiss on the cheek.

"If that's the best you two can do, you might as well forget about the wedding," Alma told Miss Joan. "I've seen more passionate pet rocks in my time," she teased.

"Huh," the woman snorted dismissively. "Some of us don't like to engage in public displays of affection." She smiled at her fiancé. "Behind closed doors, though, is a whole other story."

"Something to look forward to." Harry chuckled, his blue eyes crinkling. "Right now, though, we're here to get some of your world-famous potpie for lunch, darlin'." He began to take out his wallet.

Miss Joan placed her hand over it. "Put that away. You know your money's not any good here."

"At least let me pay for my grandson." He nodded toward the door.

Cash walked in at that exact moment. "I can pay for my own meals, Grandpa," he said. He knew his grand-father's funds were limited. The old man had given him more than a head start, paying for his first years in college. There was no way he could ever begin to repay him, but covering expenses would at least be a small start. "Besides, I should be paying for you."

"Neither one of you is paying anything. Family doesn't pay," Miss Joan insisted. "And when I marry your grandpa, here," she told Cash, patting Harry's hand, "you become my family."

Cash smiled, appreciating the sentiment. Nonetheless, he still pushed the twenty-dollar bill toward her on the counter. "Until then, I'll pay," he told her. "Call it a matter of pride."

Miss Joan ignored the bill and left it sitting on the counter. "Two chicken potpies coming up," she announced, raising her voice in order to relay the order to Roberto, the short-order cook in the kitchen.

Sitting on the other side of Harry, who was a tall, heavyset man, Alma was all but obscured. Still, she knew she was kidding herself if she thought Cash hadn't seen her as he walked in.

With her haven invaded, it was time to go.

Deliberately not looking to her right, Alma got off the stool. "Thanks for the lemonade, Miss Joan," she said, addressing the back of the woman's head.

Miss Joan swung around, doing a quick assessment. "You didn't finish it," she pointed out.

"I know, and it's very good, but I've got to be getting back to the office. I've already been gone longer than I should."

"Big crime wave to deal with?" Miss Joan arched an eyebrow as she looked at her.

Alma smiled brightly. "You never know. Nice seeing you, Harry." She nodded at the man sitting to her right. She'd always liked Harry and didn't want to seem rude.

That wasn't the case with his grandson. She barely nodded at Cash as she passed him, saying only, "You," as if it was an afterthought. She let the single word hang there without any embellishment, allowing Cash's imagination to supply any missing words he might have wanted to use.

Or not. It made no difference to her.

Alma walked out of the diner without a backward glance. The second she crossed the threshold and the door shut behind her, she quickened her pace. She wanted to get into her car and make good her escape before Cash had a chance to catch up to her.

She should have walked faster.

"Alma." She heard Cash call her name but pretended not to. He didn't give up. "Alma, wait up."

Since he'd raised his voice enough to cause several people to look their way as they walked by, she had no choice but to stop.

"Yes?" she asked coolly, turning toward him as he approached her. Her tone belied the turmoil going on inside. She felt as if everything within her was squirming. She wanted to simply get away.

"Alma, wait," he repeated, reaching her. "You don't have to leave just because I came in."

"I wasn't leaving because of you." Her tone was no longer cool. It was downright cold. "I said I had to get back to the office—"

She was lying. He knew she was lying. So, it had come to this. The most honest woman he'd ever known in his life was lying to him.

He'd done that to her, he thought with a bitter pang.

"I'll go," he told her quietly. "You stay and have your lunch. Or at least finish your lemonade." And then, because something inside him longed to reach out to her, to just *talk* to her for a moment, he said, "Still like those things, huh?"

There wasn't even a glimmer of a smile on her lips. She looked as if she was barely tolerating breathing the same air as he was. "When I like something, I stay with it. I don't see any reason not to."

"Ouch." He smiled at her then. It was a small, sad smile that struggled to filter into his eyes. "That was a direct hit," he announced, the way he might have once done when they played Battleship.

Her eyes narrowed to small, dismissive slits. "I don't know what you're talking about."

He was tired, so tired. A part of him had hoped that by coming back here, he could reclaim at least a small part of his soul. But he'd been wrong. Maybe he didn't deserve to reclaim his soul after what he'd done.

"Yes, you do," he told her softly. "We both do. You don't have to run away each time I show up." It was almost a plea.

Ordinarily, by now she would have relented, put the hurt behind her and moved on. But this hurt was too large to ignore, too large to place behind her. She'd be a fool to let it go and leave herself open to more pain. Because without the hurt to cling to and use as a shield, she'd be putting herself at risk all over again.

He was here only for the wedding. She only had to remain strong for two weeks. Just 20,160 minutes, that was all.

"You had nothing to do with it. I—" And then she stopped abruptly. Pulling her cell phone from her back pocket, she put it to her ear. "Hello?"

"I didn't hear anything," Cash said.

Covering the bottom of the phone for a second, she told him in a hushed, annoyed voice, "That's because it's on vibrate." And then she turned her attention back to the cell phone. "Right. I was just coming back. Be there in a few minutes, Sheriff. I'll take care of it then," she promised.

With that, she ended the call and slipped the phone into her back pocket again.

"Take care of what?" Cash wanted to know. She'd already begun walking away from him.

"I'm sorry, but that's on a need-to-know basis," she informed him crisply, recalling the line from a TV program she'd seen recently, "and you don't need to know."

His eyes pinned her down for a moment. "You're

lying again, aren't you? I've never known you to lie before, Alma, and now you've done it twice."

I've lied to you more than that since you came back to town, she told him silently.

She raised her chin, a clear sign that she was getting ready for a fight.

"I have no control over what you think or don't think, and frankly, I could care less." *There, another lie to add to the pile.*

With that, she turned on her heel and got into the Jeep.

She was aware that Cash was watching her. And that he continued watching her as she started up the vehicle and drove away from the diner.

Cash was right and it annoyed the hell out of her. There'd been no phone call. She'd made it up, just as she had made up the so-called conversation she'd had with the sheriff. It was the first thing that had occurred to her in her effort to get away from Cash.

At least it had worked, she congratulated herself. She'd managed to get away without becoming entangled in any kind of verbal confrontation with him.

So what did she do for the other thirteen days before the wedding? she asked herself as a feeling of uneasy desperation undulated through her.

With effort, she banked it down.

This, too, shall pass, she promised herself—and fervently hoped she was right.

Chapter Four

Sleep had eluded her for most of the night, finally descending on her at almost three in the morning. Because she was so exhausted by then, she had overslept.

Feeling as if she was running on empty, Alma rushed through her shower and into her clothes. Her stomach protested the lack of fuel, rumbling and growling as she hurried to her car.

She knew she wouldn't be of any use to anyone if she didn't have at least *something* to eat. So, with a sigh, she made a quick side trip to the diner. She was going to get an order of French toast to go. French toast was her number-one comfort food, something her mother used to make in order to cheer her up when she was a little girl. Eating it always made her remember those days and how secure she'd felt.

She needed a dose of that right now. Badly.

Miss Joan looked up the second she opened the door.

"I was hoping you'd come in today." Glancing over her shoulder, she called out to the cook in the kitchen. "Roberto, one order of French toast to go."

Alma blinked, surprised. "How did you know?" she asked.

"I know a lot of things. What I don't know," Miss Joan said, coming closer, "was what the hell that was yesterday."

Alma did her best to look innocent, hoping Miss Joan would take the hint. "What do you mean?"

"You know damn well what I mean, baby girl," Miss Joan said. "The second Harry's boy came in with him, you hightailed it out of here like some scared jackrabbit who'd just backed up into a coyote." There was both annoyance and disappointment in the woman's voice.

Alma dearly loved Miss Joan. The woman, for all her gruffness, had become like a second mother to her. But she really didn't feel like discussing the episode or anything that had to do remotely with seeing Cash again.

"I had to get back to the office." That had been her story yesterday and she was sticking to it. But it was obvious that Miss Joan wasn't buying her lie.

"You had to run out of here," Miss Joan corrected. "Now, I know he hurt you and I'm not making any excuses for him *or* excusing him, even if I am marrying his grandfather. What Cash did wasn't right, but I'm more interested in you. I've never known you to run and hide from *anything*."

"I didn't—" Alma began to protest.

Miss Joan leveled a look at her that would have had strong men confessing their sins.

"You did," she said firmly. And then her tone softened. "You want to get back at that boy, you don't run, you stand and talk to him. Make him see—and regret—just what he missed out on all these years by staying away. *That's* how you get your revenge."

But Alma shook her head. "No, I don't want any revenge."

Miss Joan put her hand over Alma's on the counter and stopped her right there. "Honey, take it from someone who's lived a lot longer. We all want revenge when we've been hurt. That's only natural. That doesn't mean it has to involve bloodshed. But it does have to involve making the other person regret what they did." Miss Joan searched her eyes, momentarily holding her in place. "Think about it," she advised.

Alma took out her wallet and paid for her order. "I will," she promised.

Roberto placed the hot breakfast, now carefully packaged and in a brown bag, on the counter between the kitchen and Miss Joan's station. Miss Joan brought it over to Alma.

With a smile, she said, "That's all I can ask for, baby girl."

"Think she'll talk to him?" Roberto asked Miss Joan the second the door closed behind Alma.

Going over to the giant coffee urn, Miss Joan dispensed another cup of coffee, her third of the morning. "I'm counting on it," she replied.

She'd made up her mind about it yesterday. She would get those two together if it was the last thing she did.

It would be her gift to Harry.

AS IF IN DIRECT CONTRAST to the way she'd rushed to make it to work on time, the pace for the rest of Alma's morning was incredibly slow. There seemed to be nothing to do, even with Larry taking the day off to attend to what he'd called "personal business." That usually translated to mean that he'd gone fishing, something the blond deputy enjoyed doing at least several times a year. Rain had been predicted for the latter half of the week, so he wasn't taking any chances on having his plans for the weekend ruined. He was taking his weekend ahead of schedule.

She supposed that all made sense to Larry.

To ward off boredom, after she'd organized everything she could in the kitchenette, Alma occupied herself by drawing up a list of things that needed to be done before Miss Joan's shower, as well as a list of things *for* Miss Joan's shower.

She, Olivia and Mona, the sheriff's wife and sister, were throwing the party for the woman. Even with there being three of them, pulling it off would be a challenge inasmuch as Miss Joan had made it perfectly clear that she didn't want a shower, or any kind of a fuss made over the coming nuptials.

Initially she'd maintained that she would have been content just living with Harry and letting things continue as they were. It was Harry, she'd said, who had insisted on this wedding. It amused her—and Alma suspected probably touched her as well—that Harry didn't want people in town thinking that the woman he loved was "living in sin" with him.

He really was rather sweet, Alma couldn't help thinking. Too bad that his grandson hadn't inherited some of his traits.

Drawing up the lists was taking her twice as long as it should have, not because she was stumped as to what to put on them, but because her mind kept wandering back to what Miss Joan had said to her this morning about the best way to exact revenge.

She was torn between following the woman's advice and just continuing the way she had.

Both sides had merit, she told herself. But only one side didn't involve a painful one-on-one with Cash. She finally just pushed it all aside, deciding that she needed to think about it later.

Because things were so slow—there hadn't even been a single phone call to report a missing pet—she volunteered to take the afternoon patrol through town in place of Joe.

Patrolling was one of Joe's least favorite parts of being a deputy.

"You sure about this?" he asked her.

Alma nodded. She needed to get out and take in some fresh air. She'd already caught herself nodding off twice since she'd gotten there.

"It's either go on patrol or fall asleep at my desk," she told him.

"Can't have that," he agreed. Digging into his pants pocket, he found the keys to the Jeep and tossed them to her. "Just make sure you don't go falling asleep behind the wheel," he warned.

"Don't worry, I won't wreck it. The sheriff would never forgive me." Looking at the keys, she murmured, "Thanks," and got up. After pushing in her chair, Alma picked up her hat—though she rarely wore it—and made her way out the door.

Maybe the fresh air *would* clear her head, she thought hopefully. God knew it couldn't do her any harm. Right now, her head felt like a battle zone and she didn't know which side she wanted to win. All she knew was that she wanted a little peace—and she knew damn well that wasn't in the cards for another twelve days.

After she'd made a complete pass through the town, rather than drive back to the office, she found herself driving to the perimeter of the town instead. Driving to the one place she always gravitated toward whenever she needed to work things out in her head.

She headed toward the cemetery.

Specifically, she was going to her mother's grave. To talk to her.

Leaving her vehicle parked at the edge of the small hundred-year-old cemetery, Alma opened the weathered wrought-iron gate.

It creaked a painful greeting at her and then creaked again as she closed it. She went directly to her mother's grave site.

Even if she didn't make it a point to visit here every Sunday, she would have easily found her way. The headstone placed on her mother's grave was, in her opinion, unique. Carved out of dark marble, there was a photograph of Anna embedded in the upper portion of the stone. It captured the way her mother had looked as a young bride.

It was, Alma's father had told her, the way he liked to remember his late wife, with the wind in her hair and a soft, happy smile on her face.

The headstone hadn't always been there. A simple cross had marked the spot for more than a year until the bills were finally paid. Then she, her brothers and her father had bought Anna Rodriguez the kind of head-stone she deserved. One as unique, as beautiful, as she had been.

Alma laid the flowers she'd stopped to buy on her way here against the headstone and then backed up a little.

"Hi, Mom, you've probably been expecting me," she said, looking at the picture. "Guess you know that Cash is back in town." She sighed. "I just don't know how to handle seeing him again. Part of me wants to scratch his eyes out and yell at him, a small part of me wants to throw my arms around him and just hold on, while a bigger part wants to avoid him like the plague. Except that I can't avoid him. His grandfather's marrying Miss Joan—can you believe it?" she interjected in a sidebar. "Miss Joan, getting married? Anyway, Cash is going to be here for the next two weeks, until the wedding. So, like it or not, I'm going to be running into him, unless he hides out at the ranch, which isn't likely.

"Miss Joan says I shouldn't give him the silent treat-

ment, that I should act the way I normally do, let him
see what he's been missing all these years.

"I don't know," she confessed. "If he thought he
was really missing something, wouldn't he have been
back before now?" The sigh she exhaled came all the
way from her toes. "I used to think that once I grew
up, I'd have all the answers." She looked at the photograph again, wishing with all her heart her mother
was actually there. To talk to her, to tell her what to
do. "Nobody told me that I'd just have more questions."
She closed her eyes for a moment, afraid that she might
start crying. "Damn him, anyway."

"I'm sorry, Alma."

Startled, she felt her heart leap up into her throat
and threaten to remain there. Half-convinced she was
imagining things, Alma swung around to look behind
her.

It wasn't her imagination.

She wished it was.

How much had he heard?

If this was autumn, she would have heard leaves
crunching under his feet as he approached, but summer
had only grass and it endured footfalls in silence. There
hadn't been anyone around when she'd entered and
she'd really thought she was alone.

God knew she wouldn't have poured out her heart
the way she just had if she'd thought that *anyone* could
overhear her, especially Cash.

"How long have you been standing there?" she said.

"Not long." It was a lie, but he didn't want to embarrass her. That wasn't why he'd made his way over after seeing her from the other side of the cemetery. "And I didn't mean to intrude. It's just that when I saw you standing there, I thought maybe I could finally get a chance to tell you how sorry I am for being such a jackass."

The apology caught her off guard and for a second, she didn't know how to respond, so she stalled and asked him a question instead. "What are you doing here?"

"I came to pay my respects to my parents. They're buried over there." He indicated a spot located beneath a tree, closer to the entrance.

How could she have forgotten that both his parents were laid to rest here? But then, he hadn't been by in all these years, and she had no reason to believe their paths would cross here. For that matter, she was surprised that he remembered where the graves were.

"You said something about being a jackass?" she prodded. Maybe it was petty of her, but she wanted to hear the rest of his apology.

Rather than dismiss his words, the way she half expected him to, he nodded. "I thought when I saw you here that I was getting a second chance to try to make amends. I should have apologized right off," he told her.

"Technically it's a third chance," she corrected. When he looked at her a little uncertainly, she clarified. "The first was in the sheriff's office yesterday. The second was later at Miss Joan's diner. That would make this the third time," she concluded.

"You're right," he agreed. "A third chance." And then he paused for a moment before continuing. "I was sorry to hear about your mother passing away." He should have been here with her for that. Maybe he should have been here all along. He wouldn't have earned any huge fees or accolades, but the Douglas family would have still been alive.

The thought almost closed his throat, choking him. "Grandpa told me," he finally explained.

She nodded. "At least you kept in touch with him." She knew that from the questions she'd asked the old man in the beginning, hungry for any news of Cash. That was back when she still thought Cash was coming back.

He knew what she was saying and he wasn't going to lie or sugarcoat it so that he could come off well. "It was more like he kept in touch with me. He wrote to me all the time," he said ruefully. The old man had never stopped, even though Cash rarely found time to answer even a tenth of those letters. "I did send him money regularly as soon as I was earning a living, but to be honest, I more or less distanced myself from that part of my life." And it made him ashamed to admit this now. Forever was the only place that seemed genuine to him, the place where people looked out for one another rather than looking to take advantage of one another.

"Yes," she said, nodding her head in response to his last words. "I noticed."

And that was his cue to apologize again, he thought.

Not that he felt he could be forgiven. But he wanted her to know, to *believe* he was genuinely sorry.

"I was an idiot and I have no excuse for behaving the way that I did," he said earnestly. "You have every right in the world to hate me."

"I don't hate you," she protested, and it was true, she didn't. Love and hate might have very well been two sides of the same coin, but she had never felt the need to flip it. "I did have the uncontrollable urge to beat on you from time to time and to give you a piece of my mind rather loudly," she admitted. "But I never hated you."

"You should have," he said. "I wouldn't blame you if you did." He wanted her to know that. That he would be perfectly understanding if she turned on him. "I let myself get sidetracked by all that gingerbread without realizing how that would hurt you."

"And yet I survived," she concluded loftily, wanting to bring an end to that line of conversation. The second he'd told her to be angry at him, she couldn't be angry any longer. His apology took the wind out of her sails and let her navigate into calmer waters.

She changed the subject. "Your grandfather said you were working for a high-profile firm. He keeps a scrapbook on you, you know."

Cash laughed softly to himself. The sound was empty. "Sounds just like him. He's a really good man," he said.

Okay, just what was going on? she wondered. The moment Cash began talking at any length, she could hear the sadness all but pulsating within his voice. And as he spoke, the pain seemed to grow deeper and deeper with each word he uttered.

Alma forgot about wanting to beat on him, forgot about how deeply hurt she'd been. Instead, what she felt now was concern.

And that had a lot to do with her inherent nature. Ever since she could remember, she had always been a sucker when it came to the hurt and the maimed. As a child, she was the one who was forever bringing home wounded animals and insisting on nursing them back to health. Usually, she did. But when she couldn't accomplish that, when the poor creature was beyond help and died on her, she would cry bitterly, mourning each and every loss.

"Your problem is that your heart is just too darn big," her father used to lament, trying to still her tears.

But she'd never seen that as being a problem.

Except for maybe now.

She knew that another woman would have seen Cash's crushed spirit, at the very least, as payback. Karma with its classic refrain of what went around came around was never more apparent than here, at this moment.

Still, she didn't think that anyone deserved to feel as much pain as Cash was apparently feeling. Because it involved feelings and they had been all but strangers these past ten years, she approached the subject carefully. "Cash, is something wrong?"

He watched her for a long moment before finally answering. "Other than my realizing how badly I treated you?"

That wasn't what she was concerned about right now. "Yes."

"No," he replied perhaps a bit too quickly, a bit too tersely as he shook his head. And then, as if sensing that she wouldn't be satisfied with just this, he added. "I'm just realizing how many wrong turns I've taken since I left Forever."

He was lying to her, Alma thought. Something else was bothering him, she would swear to it. But she couldn't exactly demand that he come clean. There was no way to force him to tell her what she wanted to know. And there was such a thing as privacy.

Besides, as compassionate as she might be, she was still coming to terms with having been one of the walking wounded herself, so right now, her mind wasn't as clear as it could be.

She suppressed a sigh. She had a little time to spare. Cash would be here until the wedding and maybe by then she could get him to level with her and say what was *really* bothering him. It had to be more than the way he'd treated her.

And if he didn't tell her, if he stubbornly maintained his own counsel, continued to live within his own eternal hell, well, he was an adult and ultimately entitled to do whatever he wanted to. All she could do was be available to him if he needed to talk.

"This probably seems quaint to you in comparison

to Los Angeles," she finally said, thinking it was a safe bet that he couldn't wait to leave again.

"Yes, it does," he agreed. And then he said something that took her completely by surprise. "There's a lot to be said for quaint."

That alone told her that there was more going on with him than he was admitting.

And then he abruptly changed the subject by looking at her, a hint of a smile curving his mouth. "A deputy, huh? I've got to admit that I never envisioned you as a deputy sheriff."

"Why not? I was always interested in criminology," she reminded him.

"I know, but I guess I thought that you were probably going to go into ranching. That criminology was, you know, like a hobby with you."

Hadn't he been paying attention the many times they'd talked about the future? Or had he just forgotten? "I guess that maybe you didn't know me as well as you thought."

"No," he agreed sadly, "I guess not."

There it was again. The bottomless sadness in his voice. In his eyes.

The hell with backing off.

That wasn't in her nature anyway. She made up her mind to talk to his grandfather. Maybe Harry knew the reason for the haunted look in Cash's eyes. She couldn't fix what she didn't understand.

And she intended to fix whatever was wrong with Cash. For old times' sake.

Chapter Five

Strange the way things arranged themselves, Alma thought as she walked back to the cemetery's front gate with Cash. If anyone would have told her last night that she would propose to help him now, she would have said they were crazy.

And yet, here she was, extending not just an olive branch but the whole damn tree. All because he'd apologized and looked so incredibly sad.

"Barring Forever's first-ever crime wave suddenly taking place, I'll be off duty at six tonight," she began, carefully measuring out each word before she said the next one. "If you don't have any kind of plans, would you like to get a cup of coffee with me?"

For a second, stunned, Cash said nothing. This was a complete one-eighty reversal from the way she'd behaved yesterday. He'd known Alma to be impulsive at times, but she had never been mercurial. Could she have really changed that much?

Why not? He had. Maybe she had, too.

Whatever the reason, he was glad she was willing to spend some time with him, even if it was at the diner, most likely under the watchful eye of his grandmother-to-be.

The corners of his mouth curved. "No, I have no plans."

They were outside the cemetery now. She noticed a cream-colored new Mercedes parked not too far from the Jeep she'd driven here. His? No one else around the area had the kind of money that the car required, which meant he had to have driven here from Los Angeles rather than flown. Why? Something to ask him tonight if there was a lull in the conversation.

"Good," she responded. "Then I'll meet you at Miss Joan's after six. We can grab a table, have some coffee." Her eyes met his. "Catch up."

Was it her imagination, or did he look just the slightest bit uncomfortable when she'd mentioned the last part?

"Sounds good," Cash agreed after a beat. "But I have to ask," he confessed, changing the course of the conversation as he walked her to her vehicle. "Why the change?"

Because you look so sad and lost. Because I could never walk away from someone who needed help—even if they weren't willing to admit it outright.

She knew that neither reason was something he would want to hear. Most likely, if she told him either one, he wouldn't show up tonight.

"I'm a female. We're allowed to change our minds. It's in our bylaws."

He shook his head and she could have sworn she

heard what sounded like a soft laugh pass his lips. She took it as a good sign.

"See you later," he told her.

"Later," she echoed, except that she made it sound more like an order.

She left first, driving away before Cash even began to head toward what she'd assumed was his car. The idea of meeting him later was creating a fluttery feeling deep in the pit of her stomach.

Just like in the old days, she thought with a pang.

Except that back in the old days, it was because she was so attracted to him and she was afraid of doing or saying something that would make her look like a fool in his eyes. This time the flutter was there because she didn't feel comfortable around him after all this time and she wondered if the conversation between them would turn into a jumble of stops and starts.

She needed to make sure that didn't happen. She'd never get to the bottom of why he looked the way he did if they couldn't talk to each other. With a wave of sadness she recalled that she had talked to the old Cash for hours on end. But this new version would be a challenge.

What she really needed was a host of topics she could refer to, picking up one if another fell flat.

Alma glanced at her watch, gauging how much time she had to prepare mentally before she saw Cash again later.

THE MOMENT SHE GOT BACK to the office, she went straight to her desk and called Cash's grandfather at home. But after twelve rings, there was still no answer. The man could be anywhere. Tending to the horses, out with Miss Joan or even doing a little shopping for a gift for the bride on her wedding day. There was no way she could reach him. He didn't have a cell phone, said he couldn't be bothered with anything like that.

He *did* have an answering machine, she recalled, an ancient one whose prerecorded message abruptly cut off before completing the sentence about leaving a name and number, but at least it worked. Not that she intended to leave a message because, with her luck, Cash would accidentally overhear it. She had a feeling he wouldn't take kindly to having her ask questions about him.

Hanging up, Alma told herself she would call back again later and keep trying until she reached Harry.

In the meantime, she would just have to use the resources that were available to her. She decided to start with the sheriff.

Getting up, she crossed over to his office. He was busy writing. By hand. Although there was a perfectly good computer on his desk and he used it when he absolutely had to, Rick still preferred the old-fashioned way: writing reports by hand. Nothing, he claimed, beat the personal touch.

She was inclined to agree with him, albeit silently.

Sensing someone was in the doorway, Rick looked up and saw her. "Something I can do for you, Alma?" he asked mildly.

She tried to sound blasé, but she had a feeling that

it was a useless attempt on her part. The sheriff was pretty good at reading people.

"I was just wondering if you knew what was going on with Harry's grandson."

Rick had always been one who called a spade a spade. He had no patience when it came to waltzing with words. He didn't dance and he expected his deputies to refrain from wasting their time and his.

"You mean Cash."

She nodded, giving up any and all attempts at sounding detached. "I mean Cash."

Rick laid down his pen and studied her face as he asked, "What's your question exactly?"

"There's something bothering Cash. He's different. Troubled, I guess, would be the best description in this case. There's a terrible sadness in his eyes and I was just wondering if maybe you either knew or could take an educated guess as to why."

"Why would I know?" Rick asked. "You're the one who's closest to him. You'd know if anyone did."

But she didn't, she thought. Alma shook her head. "I was close to him *before* he left for college. But my status changed pretty quickly. I haven't heard a word from him in years. I didn't even know he was coming back until Harry told me."

Alma took a chair without waiting for an invitation and sat down, facing the sheriff over his desk. "He's different."

Rick shrugged. He hadn't known Harry's grandson very well. They'd moved in different circles while he still lived in Forever, and besides, he was older than Cash. So all he could do was offer the logical explanation. "People change."

Maybe, but not Cash—and definitely not to this extent. "Not this much," she insisted stubbornly. "He's been through something, endured something, seen something that's taken the happiness right out of his eyes."

"Well, I can't say I noticed his eyes one way or another," Rick said. "And if you want to know what's bothering him, my suggestion is to ask."

Very simple advice. Unfortunately, it didn't work. "I did."

"And?"

"He said that there was nothing bothering him."

"Maybe there isn't," Rick said. Sometimes moods came for no reason.

She shook her head. "But I know it's something. I can feel it when I talk to Cash."

"Maybe Cash just doesn't want to burden you. *Or* he really doesn't want to talk about it. Either way, you're not going to know what it is until he's ready to tell you."

"What if he's never ready?" she pressed.

"Then, unless you're into mind reading, you don't find out."

Alma shook her head. "That's not acceptable," she said adamantly.

Rick laughed. "I had a feeling you'd say that." He seemed to think for a moment, then made another suggestion. "You know any of his friends in Los Angeles? They might be able to give you a little insight."

It was a good idea, except for one problem. "I don't know anything about his life in Los Angeles. Except for the name of the law firm where he works." And that was thanks to Cash's grandfather. Cash had stopped communicating with her long before he'd ever landed the internship with the prestigious law firm.

"Well, that's a start. Look them up and call them," he suggested. "Maybe they can give you some insight into what's bothering him—*if* there's something actually bothering him," he qualified.

"Oh, there's something bothering him. I'd bet my whole next year's salary on it." Hands braced against both armrests, she pushed herself up out of the chair. "Thanks," she said, referring to his last suggestion. "I'll do that. I'll call his firm." Although what she was going to say to them after they answered the phone, she had no idea.

Alma flashed a smile at him before she left his office. The kind of smile he hadn't seen on her lips for the past three days, he thought, ever since she'd found out that Cash was coming to the wedding.

"Glad I could help," Rick commented, although it was more to himself than to her. Alma had already left his office.

A woman with a mission, Alma went straight to the computer that she, Joe and Larry used on occasion. It was supposedly a communal computer, but for the most part, she was the only one to use it. Larry usually wound up swearing at it and Joe had no use for it, preferring to either write his reports or, on occasion, type them on the old typewriter they still kept on the bottom shelf in the supply closet.

On those rare times that something needed to be gotten out quickly, she was the one who was always recruited to get the job done. Of the three of them, she was the one equipped not so much with computer savvy as patience.

Sitting down in front of it, she turned it on, intending to access the internet. Once awakened, the computer wheezed and groaned like an asthmatic octogenarian trying to get up enough oxygen in his lungs to blow out his birthday candles.

Hearing the computer whine as it struggled to go through its paces, Joe looked in her direction, mildly curious. "What are you looking for?"

She wished she knew. Then it would be easier to find. "A needle in the haystack," she answered.

Unfazed, Joe shrugged. "Good luck."

She looked up at him, grateful that he was just letting the matter go. If Larry had been in today, she would have been subjected to an endless barrage of questions. Larry liked knowing everything about everything, never mind that it was none of his business. At times his curiosity proved to be handy, but most times, she thought, waiting for the noise coming from the computer to finally abate, it was just plain annoying.

After roughly five minutes, the computer stopped

making loud sounds and settled down to emit a steady, low hum. That was the signal for phase two: getting access to the internet and trying to get the search engine—*any* search engine—to work.

Exercising an infinite amount of patience, Alma typed, and then retyped the name of Cash's law firm in an attempt to locate it and get the phone number.

She was up to eleven attempts when it finally began to cooperate.

"I would have shot that thing by now," Joe told her truthfully, although with absolutely no emotion.

Alma couldn't help but laugh. "That's why I locked my gun in the drawer first," she told him. "Finally," she cried as the firm's website address came up on the monitor.

The next four minutes were spent trying to get *that* site to come up. When it finally did, she found the phone number on one of the first lines. She quickly began to write it down on the pad she'd brought over from her desk. She managed to copy down all but the last three numbers when the computer's internet connection mysteriously went down and the window she had just opened disappeared without a trace.

The words Not Signed On pulsed across the top of the screen.

Alma gritted her teeth together, trying hard to hold on to her temper. "If I was given to swearing," she said, tossing the words in Joe's general direction, "the air would be blue right now."

"I could swear for you," Joe offered, again without so much as cracking a smile.

He might not be smiling, but she was. He'd made her see the absurdity of it all and she was grateful to him for that.

"Not the same thing," she told him.

Blowing out a breath, she glanced down at what she'd managed to copy. She stared hard at the two empty spaces, trying to remember what had come next. This, she couldn't help thinking, would be when having total recall would be a wonderful thing.

"Okay, I think the next number was a three. That leaves only two unknown. I could start dialing, maybe I'll get lucky."

"And maybe you'll owe the sheriff your paycheck for the next three months," Joe pointed out. "You have any idea how many different combinations of numbers you'd have to try?"

Alma had always been fine when it came to ordinary math, the kind that a person needed when making change, or buying something that claimed to be discounted by twenty percent and figuring out what that came to.

But what Joe had just put to her came under the heading of statistics and that was when she and math parted company for the most part.

"Too many" was her answer.

"More like a hundred," he countered without any fanfare.

She stared at him. She didn't have to try to backtrack and check the figure to know that he was right. He always was when it came to math. What's more, the more complex the problem, the more likely that he was right in his answer.

"How do you *know* that?" she marveled.

"It's a gift," he answered simply. "Most likely you'll waste less time— and money—if you just reboot the computer and find the rest of the phone number that way."

Alma frowned deeply. "I hate it when you're right," she grumbled.

Joe came close to laughing just then. "Mona says the same thing," he told her.

"Always knew I liked her," Alma commented. Then, with a sigh, she began the process of getting the computer—and the internet—to come alive all over again.

This time it didn't take quite as long, predominately because she didn't bother doing a search. She went as directly as possible, given the machine she was working with, to the firm's website.

When the particulars came up several minutes later, she copied the last two numbers quickly, anticipating another computer glitch or freeze.

Because she'd anticipated it, it didn't happen.

Free to move the cursor about, Alma decided to look over the website.

Testimonials, accolades enumerating the number of cases the firm had collectively won—it was an impressive number—and detailing the kinds of cases they took on. The website also included a section that gave a brief biography, along with a flattering photograph, of all the junior and senior partners attached to the firm.

She had no interest in the others, but she was curious what Cash had written on his. She scrolled down to his name. He'd included the names of both his undergraduate and graduate schools. Also listed were the awards he'd received. But unlike in the other biographies, there was no mention made of where he hailed from.

But there was something written at the very bottom of his bio. Reading it gave her pause. It said: "On extended leave."

Since when were two-week vacations considered extended leaves?

Alma chewed on her lower lip. That didn't make any sense to her.

"Found what you were looking for?" Rick asked, coming up behind her from his office.

"I'm not sure," she murmured. All she knew was that she needed to get to the bottom of all this. Picking up the phone, she began dialing. "Let's see what I come up with after I call the firm."

She glanced at her watch. Making an adjustment for the time difference, she realized that it was just before lunch in Los Angeles. She still should be able to get someone. Given the size of the firm and its reputation, she assumed that the phones would be covered no matter what the lunch schedule might be.

Two rings were all it took before the line was picked up.

The formal-sounding, prerecorded female voice on

the other end gave her a series of choices and accompanying buttons to press, then told her if she knew her party's extension, she could dial it at any time.

Alma hated automated operators. Determined to speak to a live person, she kept pressing zero until one finally came on. The woman said the name of the law firm so mechanically, for a second Alma thought she'd been switched to another automated line. But then she thought she heard the woman breathing, so she decided to see if she was right.

"May I speak to CJ Taylor, please," she requested, doing her best to harness her Texas accent.

"I'm sorry," the woman on the other end said, "but Mr. Taylor is on an extended leave of absence. May I connect you to another one of our associates?"

She didn't bother saying no but went right to the heart of her call. "You mean he's on vacation?" Alma pressed.

"No," the somewhat lofty voice on the other end contradicted. She repeated, "Mr. Taylor's on an extended leave of absence."

Okay, let's approach this from another direction. "When will he be back?"

She wasn't expecting the answer she got. "I'm afraid I'm not privy to that information. I can have you speak to Mr. Wells if you like," the woman offered, mentioning one of the senior partners. "I'm sure he'll be able to help you."

With my question, or in general? "Is he taking over

Mr. Taylor's cases?" Alma asked, hoping that would lead to an answer she would find satisfactory.

"For now, yes, he is. Mr. Wells is handling some of Mr. Taylor's cases. Please hold," she instructed crisply. "I'll put you through."

Two minutes' worth of annoyingly soothing elevator music was followed by the return of the operator. "I'm sorry, Mr. Wells is on another line. I can either take down your phone number and have him call you back or let you speak to another associate."

I don't want to talk to another associate, I want someone to answer my very simple question.

She tried again. "And you don't know when Mr. Taylor is coming back?"

"We have already established that," the woman on the other end said, her voice tight. "No, I do not. Now do you want—"

What I want, you don't seem to want to give me.

That was when Alma hung up.

Chapter Six

Alma pressed her lips together as she stared down at the telephone receiver she had just replaced in its cradle.

Okay, she had a mystery on her hands. Not a mystery in the same vein as when Clarence Whitaker, a decidedly unathletic, overweight fifty-six-year-old grocery store clerk had woken up to find himself stranded eight feet off the ground in a tree after an evening of binge drinking because his wife had left him, but a mystery nonetheless.

Why had Cash taken a leave of absence from his firm instead of just a vacation? Why hadn't he told anyone at the firm when he was coming back, since he knew when the wedding was taking place?

And why hadn't he said anything, if not to her, then to his grandfather? She was certain he hadn't said anything to Harry because if he'd told his grandfather that he was here indefinitely, she *knew* that Harry would have passed the information on to Miss Joan and the woman would have in turn told her.

Why the secrecy? Or for that matter, why did Cash think he *needed* to keep all this a secret?

Something wasn't adding up. The Cash Taylor she remembered had always been as open and honest a person as could be found in the county, never mind the town.

Just what had the big city done to him?

She sensed that confronting him with questions outright wasn't the way to go. What she needed was to get Cash to relax, to unwind. To feel comfortable about being Cash again. Maybe then she could get him to *really* start talking. But she wasn't going to accomplish that alone. She needed help.

As she picked up the phone again, her fingers automatically tapped out the numbers on the keypad.

"Hello, Gabe?" she said when she heard the receiver on the other end being picked up.

Rather than a "yes" or "no" response, the voice on the other end asked, "Alma?"

"Yes."

Before she could say anything further, the voice on the other end said, "No, this is Eli. You want me to get Gabe? I just saw him out back. I can—"

She'd had five names to choose from and had guessed wrong, but in this case, one brother was as good as another. "No, that's okay, stay. I can talk to you."

"I'm honored," her brother cracked.

She could envision him placing his hand solemnly over his heart and playing this to the hilt. "Shut up and listen," she instructed. Eli had the ability to take a straight line and write an entire short story around it and she didn't have time for that right now. "Didn't you mention something about building an arch for Miss Joan and Harry's wedding? Something special for them to stand under when they exchange their vows?"

"Yeah—" It was obvious by his tone that he was waiting for a shoe—or an ax—to drop.

"Well, I got you an extra set of hands."

"Yours?" He barely stifled a laugh. "No offense, Alma, but we'll pass on that, thanks. You're pretty accident-prone. We'll spend half our time rushing you off to the hospital in the next town. And I'm pretty sure that Miss Joan and Harry won't want to exchange their vows under an arch that's got blood splattered along its perimeter, in between the flowers."

"Very funny," she commented drily. "Not me, you dummy. I'm talking about Cash. After all, he *is* Harry's grandson. I thought maybe getting him involved in doing things for the wedding would be good for him, get him to loosen up a bit. And from the way you were complaining the other day, I figured that you could use the extra help."

There was a pause on the other end, as if her brother was thinking it over. What was there to think over? They needed hands, Cash had hands. End of story.

As if, a voice in her head whispered, making her exceedingly uncomfortable. The story, she had a feeling, was just beginning.

"Sure," Eli finally answered with a careless air. "The more the better. I'll ask him the next time I run into him—*if* I run into him," he underscored.

"He'll be at the diner after six," Alma immediately volunteered.

"Okay. *When* I run into him," Eli said, amending his previous statement. Since Alma had brought up the subject of Cash, he felt it was safe to ask her a question that had him concerned. "And while we're on the subject, how are you holding up?"

"Holding up?" she repeated innocently. "What d'you mean?"

In response, she heard Eli laugh. "You're a hell of a lot of things, Alma, and you can hold your own with the best of them, but I'd give up any thoughts of being an actress if I were you. That was about as stiff a delivery as I've ever heard," he critiqued. And then his voice softened a bit. "C'mon, kid," he coaxed. "This is me, Eli. Talk to me. How are you holding up?" he asked.

This time she was the one who paused before answering. Taking in a long breath, Alma finally said, "I'm okay, Eli. Thanks for asking. But really, all that's in the past. Whatever there was between Cash and me is long gone."

"So then why this sudden interest in recruiting him for a work crew? Is the big-city lawyer bored already?" he asked.

She found herself growing protective of Cash. Protective of a man who had all but issued her her walking papers so long ago. She should have her head examined, Alma thought.

But there was no changing her. She knew that as well as anyone.

"No," she told Eli, "but I think the big-city lawyer's dealing with something he won't talk about. I'm just trying to get him to remember that he's among friends."

Eli laughed softly.

"Never could stand anyone keeping anything from you, could you, kid?"

"This doesn't have anything to do with me," she informed her brother in what he'd come to refer to as her "deputy voice," the voice of cool authority. "This is to help him—and you. A win-win situation from where I'm standing. Don't forget, he'll be at the diner after six. Be there." With that, she hung up.

"The hell it doesn't have anything to do with you," Eli said to the receiver in his hand.

CASH HAD FORGOTTEN JUST how dirty he could get, doing chores on the ranch.

Forgot, too, how good it felt doing those chores. Working with his hands. Putting his back into it.

Being a lawyer required just as much stamina as being a rancher did, but, depending on the choice, different parts of a man were called into action. The long hours he put in at the firm left him feeling drained and exhausted beyond words mentally, but he had to admit that it was just as satisfying—and maybe a little more so—to do ranch work, which left him *physically* exhausted.

He liked putting himself out there, pitting himself against the land as well as the horses his grandfather raised.

Cash had gotten so caught up with helping his grand-father's two ranch hands that he'd completely lost track of time. So much so that before he knew it, he had less than half an hour to meet Alma at the appointed time at the diner.

Which would have been no problem if he'd taken off right then, but he couldn't. Couldn't very well walk into the diner smelling like a man who'd been cleaning out stalls, among other things, all afternoon. So he'd stopped to take a very quick shower.

Which, perforce, still made him late.

As he drove to town, doing ten to fifteen miles over the speed limit, he wondered if she'd wait, or just assume he wasn't coming and leave.

When Alma had suggested that they grab a cup of coffee together this afternoon, he'd felt relief and maybe just a glimmer of hope for the first time since he'd heard the news bulletin that had sent his life into a spi-raling, devastating tailspin.

Not that he was about to get carried away, or even really feel anything significant enough to register. On an emotional scale of zero to ten, his emotions were all hovering at zero.

Because he wanted them to.

Everything inside of him was still on lockdown. That was the only way he knew of to survive. If he opened himself up, if he allowed his emotions to come out, he had a feeling that, most likely, he would wind up having a complete meltdown. The guilt that he was so desperately trying to avoid would push forward and consume him, swallowing him up whole.

As it was, right now, it was a constant battle to keep it all at bay. To not allow himself to think about what he was ultimately responsible for.

Lockdown was his only hope.

Still, he couldn't help thinking, Alma belonged to a time when life had been easier to deal with and far less complicated.

A time, he knew, he had deliberately turned his back on. And hurt people.

Hurt Alma.

Because of that, he didn't deserve to revisit that period, but that, even more than his grandfather's upcoming wedding, was why he was here. Not to recapture that time, because he knew that was impossible, but he wanted to try to remember what he'd felt, what he'd *been* like back then, if only for a few minutes.

That, too, would help him in his attempt to survive.

Hair still damp, the fresh clothes he'd put on sticking to a body that wasn't quite dried off, Cash walked into the diner. He scanned the area, looking for Alma as he took a few tentative steps forward.

At first, he didn't see her. He was twenty minutes late, despite the quick shower and all but dashing into his clothes still wet.

He should have called to tell her that he was running late, Cash scolded himself. Alma probably thought he'd stood her up or changed his mind. Not that he could blame her. After all, it wasn't as if he'd behaved dependably toward her.

And then he saw her coming out from the rear of the diner. She was busy talking to one of the waitresses, but her eyes met his and she nodded. Relieved, unaware of the fact that he was actually smiling broadly, Cash made his way over to her, an apology ripe on his lips.

"Hi," he greeted her the moment he was close enough not to have to shout. "I was afraid you'd left. Sorry I'm late." The two sentences ran together.

Alma turned away from the waitress and allowed herself to take full measure of him, her eyes traveling over the length of his body. It wasn't her imagination. He really *was* wet.

"Is it raining?" she asked.

The sky had appeared threatening all day and there had been a couple of rumbles of thunder, but apparently that was just Mother Nature's way of teasing the people in this region, all of whom were praying for rain. It had been a long time in between downpours. The land was significantly parched and dry, and the ground was beginning to crack in places, as if opening itself up in hopes of being able to absorb water if it *should* happen to rain. These days, the grass was sparse and brown more often than it was green. And the price of the hay used to feed the horses had gone up. Again.

Maybe he should have taken another couple of minutes to dry off properly, Cash thought. "No, why?"

"Your hair's all wet." As she spoke, she touched his hair to see if it was as wet as it looked—it was. "And you don't look altogether dry, either," she concluded. "What happened?"

The shrug he gave in response was almost self-conscious and so reminiscent of the young man he'd once been, she couldn't help thinking. The one who'd owned her heart so completely.

"I was working in the barn, mucking out the stalls, and I guess I lost track of time. I didn't want you to think I was standing you up, but I didn't think you'd want to sit opposite me smelling the way I did, so I stopped to take a quick shower."

The thought of his rushing on her account made her smile. Maybe in a way, she still mattered to him. At least a tiny bit.

"I would have made sure I sat upwind of you," Alma assured him. For a second, her eyes held his. "But I do appreciate the thoughtfulness."

She turned to glance over her shoulder. Just as she suspected, Miss Joan was making no secret of the fact that she was watching them. "We'll have that coffee now, Miss Joan."

The woman nodded. "Just sit yourselves at that table," Miss Joan instructed, pointing toward the one that Alma had been occupying before she'd gotten up to talk to one of the waitresses. "I'll have two cups of coffee there for you before you know it," she promised.

Alma led the way back. Cash tried not to let his eyes dip down to watch her as her hips moved to a silent rhythm only she was unaware of, but he couldn't seem to help himself. Working hard and then rushing had worn down his resolve.

"So your grandfather put you to work, did he?" she asked once they reached the table and she sat down.

Cash slid into the booth opposite her. "Actually, I had to beg him to let me. He said this was my vacation and I should just kick back, but I convinced him that I really wanted to lend a hand. I'd forgotten how satisfying it is to work with your hands. And," he confessed, "how backbreaking." As if to underscore his point, he rotated his shoulders. "I've got places starting to ache that I'd forgotten I even had."

He was wearing a work shirt, its sleeves rolled up. She could see veins and definition along his forearms. It reminded her of the way he'd looked that last summer. "That's because you're not used to it."

"It's not like I just sit behind a desk all day and don't move," he protested.

She cocked her head, a smile playing on her lips. "They have you jumping over the bar to get into the courtroom, do they?"

"I meant I belong to a gym," he clarified. "I work out whenever I can."

Yes, she could believe that. He still cut an impressive figure, but it wasn't exactly the same as when he'd lived here among them.

"You use a different set of muscles working on a ranch," she pointed out.

"Don't I know it," Cash groaned. Again he rotated his shoulders, trying to undo the knot he felt growing between his shoulder blades. And there was a stiffness along his shoulders that promised to give him a lot of trouble by this evening.

He noticed that Alma was doing her best not to grin. "It'll probably be worse tomorrow," she predicted.

"Something to look forward to," he muttered under his breath.

Miss Joan approached their table just then, holding a steaming mug of coffee in each hand. She placed one down in front of each of them. She looked in absolutely no hurry to retreat.

She'd managed to catch the last part of their conversation and made no attempt to appear as if she hadn't been listening. After all, that was what she did. How else could she help and advise people?

"Why don't you give Cash a massage after you're done here?" she suggested to Alma. She nodded toward the back office, a small cubbyhole that was crammed with various things she felt might be useful. "I've got some liniment you can use." Her eyes swept over Cash and then back to Alma. "Might help."

That would require touching him, Alma thought. Touching his bare skin. The flood of memories would be more than she could handle right now.

Survival instincts kicked in and Alma began to demur, "I don't think—"

Miss Joan looked at her pointedly. "I'm getting married to Harry in a few days. Harry's Cash's grandfather. That'll make Cash my grandson and my family." Miss Joan tried not to dwell on the way the word *family* made her feel, instead plowing on. "I'd take it as a personal favor if you took a little pity on the boy, see what you could do to alleviate his misery, Alma."

Cash didn't have to look at her to sense Alma's reluctance. He shook his head. "I'm fine, Miss Joan," he protested. "Really."

Miss Joan gave him a look that said she knew better. "That grimace on your face doesn't say you're fine, boy, but have it your way." She shrugged her thin shoulders. "The offer still stands, though. Got the liniment right there in the back office," she added by way of a reminder as she walked off.

Alma hesitated. "Look, if you're really in a lot of pain—" she began.

"No, it's okay." He didn't want her to feel that she was on the spot because of Miss Joan. He didn't want Alma doing anything that made her uncomfortable. Besides, maybe having her spreading liniment on his aching shoulders wasn't the best idea—for either of them. "I'm sure I'll get used to it. Like you said, just a different set of muscles being exercised."

"Okay," she agreed, making use of the opening he'd afforded her. "Then maybe you're up for more of those muscles being exercised."

"What d'you mean?" he asked, surprised.

The look on his face told her that perhaps she hadn't exactly worded her last statement correctly. "I was just asking if you were open to a little more physical work." *Yeah, that's a big improvement,* she mocked herself. She spoke more quickly. "My brothers and the sheriff are working on a wedding arch for your grandfather and Miss Joan. You know, someplace for them to stand along with the minister and exchange their vows. Eli mentioned that he could use some help so I told him that I'd ask you if you wanted to pitch in since it was for your grandfather and all," she added, watching his face.

For a second, her words had his thoughts taking him someplace else. Why he would think that she was suggesting that they get together in *that* way was beyond him. He'd burned that bridge behind him the minute he'd gone across it and away from her.

Chagrined, he said, "Sure, count me in."

Can't act, huh, Eli? Alma thought, feeling rather smug about the performance she'd just given, making Cash think the idea to pitch in had been Eli's and not hers. *In your face, big brother.*

Chapter Seven

Sitting in the diner across from Cash, the din swelling around them as they talked, for just a moment Alma basked in the feeling that this was just like old times.

Or as close times as she was probably going to get.

They'd finished only a little less than half their coffees—each was just sipping the dark liquid almost as an afterthought while they talked—when Eli walked into the diner.

Or when he sauntered into the diner, that was probably a better description for it, Alma thought.

She could see several women look in her brother's direction, their words obviously momentarily suspended in midair or on their tongues as they let their imaginations roam a bit on the wild side before continuing with their lives.

Her big brother would break a lot of hearts when he finally got married.

Alma was quick to raise her hand in the air, trying to catch her brother's attention.

"Hey, Eli," she called out to him. "Over here." She

beckoned him over. "Come join us. You don't mind, right?" she asked Cash belatedly.

"No, I don't mind," he said quietly.

Eli Rodriguez had once been his best friend, but since Eli was also Alma's brother, he had broken any connection to his friend, as well. At the time, he'd told himself that it was for the best.

The only tie he hadn't severed was that with his grandfather.

The man, he couldn't help thinking, who had tried to keep him grounded. But no one could tell him anything back then after he'd had his first taste of big-city life, least of all that he would come to regret breaking with everything that was real in life.

Eli strode hesitantly over to their booth, as if not sure how to act.

Cash eliminated the awkwardness by immediately initiating the conversation. "Alma said you need an extra hand building the wedding arch."

Eli's eyes darted over toward the counter to make sure that Miss Joan, with her batlike hearing, hadn't overheard Cash's remark.

"Yes, we do," he said as he slid in next to his sister in the booth and faced Eli. "Two hands if you can spare them," he cracked. And then he lowered his voice, "But if you don't mind, don't say anything about this to your grandfather—or Miss Joan. It's supposed to be a surprise."

"Oh." Cash looked at Eli's sister. "Alma didn't mention that part."

"Alma didn't know that part," Alma said in her own defense, looking at Eli. "You never said anything about it being a surprise."

"I just assumed you'd figure that part out. Sorry, I guess I should have known better," Eli told her, doing his best to keep a straight face.

"What you should have done was *said* something," she corrected. "I'm not a mind reader, Eli, even if the mind is as simple as yours."

Cash looked from Eli to Alma and shook his head, amusement flittering ever so slightly into his somber features. "Well, I see nothing's changed."

And once, when he was just getting started at the firm in L.A., he knew he would have thought that sameness was off-putting and hokey. Instead, now he found it to be oddly reassuring. Like a child uncovering something familiar to cling to in the middle of a violent storm, he couldn't help thinking.

"What do you mean?" Alma asked. There was a trace of defensiveness rising in her voice as she braced herself for a put-down.

"You and Eli are still at it, ragging on one another," Cash told her. Although he knew she loved all her brothers fiercely and was the first to jump to their defense, Alma had always been very competitive when it came to her brothers. She never wanted to be thought of as lacking in any area, never wanted to be left behind in any race. "Are you still like that with the rest of your brothers?"

"If you're asking if they try my patience, yes, they

do," she answered, pausing to take another sip of her coffee which was now growing cold. "Otherwise, I haven't got the faintest idea what it is that you're talking about," she sniffed.

"Never mind her for now," Eli said, waving a dismissive hand at his sister. "You think you can come over to the ranch tomorrow and give us some help for a couple of hours? Any time you can spare, swinging a hammer or manning a saw, would be much appreciated. We're cutting it kind of close," he admitted.

"Sure, anything I can do to help," Cash heard himself agreeing. It felt almost liberating, he thought. But then, working with his hands always was a great way to relieve his stress.

Initially, he'd just planned to come back to Forever to attend the wedding. For the most part, he had intended to stand back like an observer in someone else's life. It would be an attempt on his part to get a handle on things and maybe, if he was lucky, to take comfort in the fact that some places in the country—specifically his hometown—hadn't changed.

It was his secret hope that watching the world he'd once known go through its paces—would somehow heal him.

Or, if not heal at least help him not to feel as if he'd already died and just hadn't the good sense to lie down. The hollowness he had been feeling was slowly eating him up alive. A man could survive only so long feeling the way he did.

That was when he'd decided to come back earlier.

Because he needed to be here. Needed help just in getting through the day. Being in familiar surroundings ever so subtly provided that help.

"Then we'll see you at the ranch tomorrow," Eli said with a wide smile. "Say about nine?"

Cash thought a second, then requested, "Make it ten. I'm helping my grandfather clean out the stalls. If I back out on that after one day, I have a feeling I'd be disappointing him."

"Then you don't know your grandfather," Alma interjected. "Trust me. Nothing you could do would make him be disappointed in you. You're the center of his universe."

Even after all the distancing he'd done, Cash silently marveled, the old man still greeted him with open arms. Still made him feel welcomed. In a way, it made him feel worse because he'd neglected the old man so much, sending money regularly, but not giving him nearly enough of his time or attention.

"And I'm about to be replaced by Miss Joan," he pointed out with a forced smile.

He realized he'd felt a salvo of what oddly felt like a smattering of jealousy.

This was ridiculous. He couldn't possibly be jealous of a woman who had often described herself as being older than dirt, and while she wasn't *that* old, Miss Joan wasn't exactly younger than springtime, either. He was glad his grandfather had someone in his life. The man deserved to be happy.

He supposed his feelings arose from the fact that he

desperately didn't want to find that things had changed here. Not in the place that he realized he thought of as his haven.

Grow up, Taylor, he ordered silently. *You're acting like a naive kid.*

Just as Eli was about to get up and take his leave, Miss Joan approached their table, her attention focused entirely on him.

"Can I do anything for you, handsome?" the woman asked.

Eli grinned at her. "Yes, you can call off your wedding to Harry and run away with me."

Miss Joan shook her head as if taking his words seriously. "Oh, Eli, if only you'd asked a little sooner—I'm afraid that it's too late now. If I run away with you, it would break Harry's heart. Besides, you're too young for me."

"Only by a couple of years," Eli answered, keeping a straight face. "And truth be told, you're almost too much woman for me."

"As if that was possible." Miss Joan laughed. And then she patted Eli's shoulder. "You're good for me, Eli. You make me feel young."

"You *are* young, Miss Joan," Alma chimed in, and she was serious. There was no one quite like Miss Joan. The woman was definitely one of a kind. "You know you're younger than all of us."

"No, not younger," Miss Joan contradicted. "But I am experienced. I just know that whatever's wrong isn't going to stay wrong. And if it does, you still find a way to move on. Moving targets are harder to hit," she said, taking in all three of them as she winked.

And then she sashayed away, back to her place behind the counter.

Watching her leave, Cash shook his head in amazement. "I think my grandfather's going to have his hands full," he commented.

"I'm still kind of surprised that he got her to say yes," Eli confided. "No offense to your grandfather, but Miss Joan's always been cagey about commitments, at least for as long as I've known her."

"Which is *so* much longer than the rest of us have known her," Alma teased. "You're only three years older than I am and two years older than Cash."

"Older is older," Eli maintained.

Alma rolled her eyes. "Very profound, Eli," she deadpanned. "Remind me to have that put on a T-shirt sometime."

Rather than respond, Eli looked at Cash instead. "If she gets on your nerves—and I can't see how she can't—you know where to find me."

"Actually," Cash told him, a little chagrined, "I don't."

Eli took his friend's confession in stride. "I'm still living on the family ranch. Makes it easier to work the place," he explained.

"How about you?" Cash asked Alma. "Are you still living at the ranch, too?"

"No, I moved out three years ago when I started

working full-time. I'm living in town now," she told him. "So I can be close by if the sheriff needs me."

"Don't let her fool you," Eli told his friend. "She just doesn't want to get roped into helping out at the ranch, not after putting in a *hard day* keeping the peace. Right, Alma?"

Alma looked at her brother pointedly. "I thought you said you were leaving."

"And so I am," Eli told her. He turned to look at Cash. "Nice seeing you again, Cash. I'll be watching for you tomorrow."

"You're smiling," Alma observed after her brother left the diner.

Her remark caught Cash by surprise. For a second, he'd let his mind drift back to when he and Eli had hung out together as boys. Back to the present, he looked at Alma, puzzled. "What?"

"I said you're smiling. No, don't stop," Alma cried when she saw the smile fade away again. "That was an observation, not a criticism. I was starting to worry that maybe you forgot *how* to smile."

"It isn't a matter of forgetting," he told her honestly, thinking of the twists his life had taken in the past five months. "It's a matter of not being able to."

The hell with biding her time and waiting. This had to be put out into the open *now*.

"Okay, I can't keep this in anymore," she said with feeling. "What happened to you, Cash?" When he made no attempt to answer her question, she put her hand over his on the table and pleaded, "Talk to me."

The entreaty coaxed forward a sliver of a smile, but Cash had no intention of answering her question. Still, rather than just brush it off, the way he had earlier, he told her, "Maybe someday, Alma. But not now."

It was obvious to him that the good people of Forever didn't pay much, if any, attention to news stories that occurred outside of their county, much less outside the state. That, too, hadn't changed. The only news they listened to was local news. Otherwise, he was certain, someone within Forever would have brought the news story to his grandfather's attention. After all, his name had been mentioned in all the major articles covering the story.

No one had actually come out and *said* that he was responsible for what had happened, but in the end, that didn't really matter. *He* felt he was responsible and there was no way he could atone for it.

No way except to give up being an attorney.

But then, if he did that, what did he do with the rest of his life? After these two weeks were over, after his grandfather was happily married and on his way to a new chapter in his life, just *what* did he do? How was he going to earn a living if he gave up the only career he knew?

And yet, if he went back to the law, went back to working for the firm, could he live with himself? Could he survive the day-to-day reminders?

"Earth to Cash, Earth to Cash."

It wasn't until Alma waved her hand in front of his face that he realized he'd let his mind drift off again and that Alma was trying, in a broadly exaggerated manner, to get his attention.

He focused on her and not his thoughts. "Sorry," he apologized.

"No reason to be sorry," Alma insisted, absolving him of any transgression he thought he'd committed. After all, she wasn't *that* thin-skinned. But she couldn't resist adding, "But if you *do* want to make it up to me, you can do it by telling me what the hell is going on in your head."

He laughed softly, shaking his head. Why had he ever walked away from her? She was more real than the entire office of people he'd worked with every day up until a week ago.

"Nice try."

"But obviously not good enough to loosen that tongue of yours," she said with a resigned sigh. "You always could be so closemouthed when you wanted to be."

Back then, she knew he did it to bait her and drive her crazy. But he always relented in the end and came clean. This, however, was different. And—she had a growing, uneasy hunch—extremely serious.

"Believe me," Cash said slowly, "you don't want to know."

It was her turn to laugh. There was a tinge of disbelief in her eyes when she looked at him.

"I guess you don't remember me at all, do you?" she asked him. "Because if you did, you would remember that I *always* want to know."

Cash looked at her for a long moment. The growing noise all around them as more and more customers came into the diner faded into the background as he debated with himself.

He had to admit that there was a small but urgent need within him to share, to unburden himself and perhaps even cleave, if only for a second, to someone's words of absolution. But that wouldn't last, he knew. His feelings of guilt were just too great.

Besides, what if there were no words of absolution, even perfunctory ones? What if she looked at him with horror and revulsion? He knew he wouldn't be able to bear that.

"No," he finally replied firmly, "you don't." Then, trying to bridge the gap that had opened up between them, he sought some neutral ground. "But you can fill me in on what's been going on here since I left," he told her.

Just like that, huh? Don't think I don't know what you're doing. You're trying to divert my attention. I don't get distracted that easily, Cash.

Out loud, she asked, "Chronologically, alphabetically or just the highlights?"

That was Alma, all right, he thought, ready to accommodate in any way that suited a person. He'd forgotten about that trait, and how much it endeared her to him.

Mesmerized by the seductive promise of a future beyond his wildest imagining, he'd completely forgotten what he'd been blessed with right here in his own backyard, Cash thought.

"Any way you want to do it," he told her. "I'll leave it up to you."

Alma nodded, settling back in the booth. "Okay, I'll give you the highlights, then."

She spent the next half hour filling Cash in on some of the more pertinent events of the past ten years that she thought he might find interesting. She told him that Rick Santiago had gotten married to a lawyer named Olivia who had come into town, tracking down her runaway younger sister. Olivia now had a practice in town, as well as a brand-new baby girl.

Rick's sister, Ramona, meanwhile, had married Joe Lone Wolf, who along with Larry—and her—comprised the sheriff's deputies. Oh, and the town had gotten their very own doctor, Dr. Daniel Davenport, after doing without one for more than thirty years. And the sheriff's sister-in-law, Tina, the same woman who was indirectly responsible for the sheriff finding a wife, wound up marrying that doctor. She was also the town bookkeeper.

Alma mentioned the babies who had been born, sticking only to people she was certain he still remembered.

As Alma went on with her annotated summary, Miss Joan came by and refilled their coffee mugs twice. The second time she brought them each a large piece of apple-caramel pie, as well.

There was whipped cream all but obliterating the piece she placed in front of Cash.

She'd remembered how he liked it, Cash thought, surprised.

As Alma continued filling him in, Cash listened and couldn't help thinking that a great deal of life had gone by while he'd been out on the West Coast, defending people the rest of the world regarded as criminals, searching for the one loophole or elusive piece of evidence that would set them free.

Whether or not those clients he represented were innocent was another story, one he couldn't allow himself to hear. Because if he knew for a fact that his client was guilty, then he wouldn't have been able to defend them. It went against his code.

But you knew, deep down in your gut, you knew Harper was guilty, a voice in his head taunted him. *Knew it even as you pounded away at that one so-called piece of evidence until you got the judge to see things your way and rule it as inadmissible.*

And got Harper to walk away scot-free.

If you just hadn't been as good as you were, as clever as you were, Harper would have gone to jail for his crimes.

And that family of five would have still been alive today.

The thought haunted his every waking moment. Sleeping was even worse.

"Have I bored you into a coma?" Alma finally asked when Cash didn't say anything, or even make any response, for several minutes. She peered at him, waiting for him to answer.

He was doing it again, he thought. Letting his mind wander—or maybe *torture* would be a better word. He was letting his mind torture him.

But then, he deserved it.

Out loud, Cash addressed her question. "No, sorry, I was just thinking."

"About?" she pressed.

The smile she saw on his lips was small, as if he couldn't muster the energy to allow anything larger to exist. Just like the look in his eyes, it echoed of sadness.

"About how many things have happened here while I was out on the coast, working," he lied.

He'd delivered the lie smoothly, Alma thought, granting him that. But she was still unconvinced, positive there was more to it than just that. His eyes told her there was.

Somehow, she thought, feeling frustrated, she had to get Cash to trust her enough to open up.

But how?

Chapter Eight

She held out for a little more than two days.

Summoning all the inner strength she had to tap into, reserved or otherwise, Alma did *not* pick up a phone or drive by the family ranch to see how Cash was doing, or find out if he so much as even showed up, or if he'd decided to back out at the last moment.

But when she accepted that all her thoughts congregated around the question of whether or not Cash had joined her brothers on the project, she finally surrendered and told Rick that she was taking one of her personal days.

"I've got to get things ready for Miss Joan's shower," was the official excuse she gave him, hoping that he didn't remember she was but one of the women involved in this and that for the most part, Rick's wife, sister and sister-in-law were the movers and shakers behind that little get-together.

To her relief, Rick didn't question her excuse in any way.

All he said was, "It's your personal day, Alma. You don't have to give me a reason you're taking it—not that

I don't appreciate being kept in the loop," he added with a smile.

And then she saw the look in his eyes. It told her that he was onto her.

Or maybe that was just her guilty conscience, making her paranoid. She *really* didn't like to lie, but somehow, admitting that she wanted to see how things were going with the building of Miss Joan's wedding arch—specifically, how *Cash* was coming along with it—made her feel as if she was just leaving herself open for unsolicited advice.

She didn't need anyone telling her that she shouldn't become so vulnerable around Cash. That rekindling so much as a spark of what they'd once had was asking for trouble, not to mention heartache.

Alma didn't need anyone saying that to her. She knew that, and didn't intend to let any of it happen. She was just worried about Cash—as a friend, nothing more.

Nothing more, she silently insisted with feeling as she drove to the family ranch.

She could hear them working long before she could see them as she approached the ranch house. The sound of hammering, laced with intermittent cursing coming from behind the barn, left no question as to where all the action was taking place.

Leaving her vehicle parked in front of the house, she made her way behind the barn, hoping to be able to observe everyone for a moment or two before anyone noticed she was there.

For all the noise she'd heard, she was surprised to see that only two of her brothers, Gabe and Rafe, were there, working alongside Cash.

Cash was the first to see her. He paused, taking the opportunity to wipe away the sweat from his brow with the back of his wrist.

"Where's your deputy uniform?" he asked, mildly surprised to see her. He'd just assumed that she had no time to pitch in and if she had, that she would have said something.

It surprised him, too, to discover just how happy he was to see her. The next moment, he banked that feeling, afraid of what it might ultimately do to him. Feeling *anything* could very well open the Pandora's box he'd worked so hard at keeping closed.

Prepared for another mercilessly hot day, Alma was wearing jeans that were threadbare in more than a couple of places, allowing for its share of ventilation to pass through the material, and a light tank top the same color as her eyes.

What she *wasn't* prepared for was the sight of Cash with his shirt tied around his waist like an afterthought, his upper torso bare and gleaming with sweat spread out over rock-hard pectorals and an abdomen that could have doubled as a rock quarry.

When had he gotten those abdominal muscles?

He'd always been muscular, but this was an entirely new plateau.

It didn't seem fair that he had only gotten better looking. Being a lawyer was supposed to make you soft. The only thing that was soft right now were her knees.

"Home, on a hanger," she answered when she finally located her tongue. Clearing her throat, she nodded at his bare chest. "Where's your shirt?"

He picked up one of the sleeves and held it up for her to see in case it escaped her. "Right here." He dropped the sleeve again. It dropped, all but reaching down to his calf. "Don't they frown on you being out of uniform?" he asked.

"Only if I'm not wearing anything in place of it," she said brightly. *Like you right now.* "It's my day off," she told him.

"Then stop talking and grab a hammer," Gabe called out, walking over to her. Her brother waved the hammer in his hand back toward the arch. "This thing isn't building itself and it's turning out to be a lot more complicated than it looked in that picture you showed us," Gabe informed her.

Cash looked at her in surprise. "So this was your idea?"

Now that he thought of it, this kind of thing was right up her alley. But she hadn't taken any credit for it when she'd initially mentioned his joining in to help build it.

"I thought it was a nice touch," she told Cash. Feeling something igniting in the pit of her stomach, she was doing her best to keep her distance from him. But she knew that really wasn't going to be possible, not if she intended to lend a hand and work on the project today. Not without her making it painfully obvious, at any rate.

"Less talking, more working," Gabe ordered.

Because it might be a good distraction as far as Cash was concerned, she decided to bait Gabe a little. "Eli said he didn't want me helping out. He said I was too accident-prone."

Gabe frowned at the excuse. "Well, Eli's not here now, is he?" he asked, gesturing around.

"Besides, we're onto you, Alma," Rafe spoke up. Hot, he stopped working for a minute and took a can of beer out of the cooler he and Gabe had brought out and placed in what little shade they could find. He pulled the top and fizz instantly clustered about the opening, pushing its way out and then the next moment, back down again.

"Oh?" She turned to face Rafe. "And just what's *that* supposed to mean?"

Rafe took a long swig of the beer, then set down the can beside the cooler. "It means that you just *act* like you're accident-prone so you can get out of working on the projects you rope the rest of us into."

"Not true," she protested. "Besides, I've done my share around the ranch."

Rather than spending any more precious time arguing with his sister, Gabe walked up to her and handed her a hammer. "You can work on the platform," he told her.

Her eyebrows drew together in surprise. This was

something new. "You're building a platform, too? When did that happen?"

"When Eli decided that it would be a nice touch to have Harry and Miss Joan stand on it as they said their vows. He said he wants the platform to be about four inches high and—well, here's the sketch he made." Reaching into his back pocket, he pulled out a greatly creased piece of paper and unfolded part of it.

"You ask me, he's just a frustrated architect," Rafe commented, adding in his two cents.

Being an architect was a dream that their brother had given up in order to move back home and help out when their mother took a turn for the worse.

If he'd felt he was giving up something Eli never said a word. None of them wanted to see their father forced to sell the family ranch. Especially since it had been in the family for three generations.

When the bills were finally paid off, their father had taken them to a lawyer in the next town and officially changed the deed to the ranch to be in all their names. They'd tried to talk him out of it, but he remained firm, saying that if it hadn't been for their combined efforts, the ranch would have been sold to pay off the debt.

Flattening the paper with her hands, Alma studied the sketch that Gabe had given her. After a moment, she could visualize the nuts and bolts of the drawing, seeing what needed to be done in order to make it a viable construction.

Folding it in half and handing it back to Gabe, she

said, "We're going to need a lot more lumber than what you've got here."

"Way ahead of you," Rafe told her. "Eli picked some up yesterday when he was in town. It's in the back of the barn." Rafe turned to Cash. "Why don't you and the little foreman here—" he nodded at his sister "—haul it over here?"

"Sure," Cash readily agreed, setting down his hammer and wiping his hands against the back of his jeans.

"By the way, where are Mike and Ray?" she asked, referring to her two other brothers who were apparently missing.

"They're out with Eli and Dad, working on that broken stretch of the fence in the lower forty before the horses decide to make a break for it," Gabe answered. "I know that it might have slipped your mind, what with all these fancy flowers around and whatnots, and you being gone most of the time, being the sheriff's little helper, but this *is* a working ranch."

She pinned her brother with a piercing look. "Well, someone certainly woke up on the wrong side of the pig trough," she commented. "What happened? Erica finally come to her senses and decide she could do better?"

Gabe looked at her for a long moment, then rather than a snappy comeback, he just said, "Yes," and turned, walking back to the half-finished arch.

She'd only meant to pull his chain, the way they did with one another. She hadn't thought she had stumbled across the truth. Remorse instantly flooded through her.

"Oh, Gabe, I'm so sorry. I didn't mean to make you feel that—"

Gabe waved a hand at her to halt her apology before she could get carried away. "Yeah, I know."

"You can do better, you know," she told him, coming up beside her brother. She reached up in order to be able to place a hand on his shoulder to comfort him. "She really wasn't good enough for you," Alma said with feeling.

Glancing at his sister, the corners of his mouth curved in a slight smile that told her it was going to take some time, but he would be all right. This wasn't the love of his life that he'd lost, just a temporary blow to his ego.

He indicated the barn. "Just go get that lumber with Cash."

With a nod, Alma retreated. Gabe knew she wouldn't have intentionally hurt him and she silently promised to find a way to make it up to him. Turning around, she saw that Cash was standing only a couple of feet away, watching her.

She couldn't begin to read the expression on Cash's face. Did what Gabe had just said remind him of something? Was the reason he seemed so sad because some woman had broken his heart?

The thought hadn't occurred to her until now. She could be trying to help mend his bruised ego and aching heart—and wouldn't that be a kick in the head?

You're doing it again, she chided. *You're leaping to conclusions and getting carried away.*

"What?" she asked as she came up to Cash. Maybe he'd actually tell her what was bothering him if she asked him enough times.

His answer in this case was *not* what she expected to hear. "You're still trying to take care of everyone, aren't you?"

She shrugged. "It's not something I think about. Just something that happens. A reaction, I guess. I've always felt that you're *supposed* to take care of your own," she told him simply. Okay, this wouldn't go anywhere right now and as Gabe had said, the arch—and the platform—wouldn't build themselves. "Let's get that wood," she coaxed, "and build this thing before your grandfather and Miss Joan celebrate their tenth anniversary."

"You always did have a way with words," he said with a laugh as he followed her inside the barn.

ALMA TURNED HER HEAD AND looked at Cash. "Think they'll be happy?" Alma asked Cash.

It was almost twilight and, too exhausted to walk into the main house for supper, she'd opted to lie on the ground for a few minutes to regroup. She was acutely aware that she was lying on dirt rather than the grass that had once been there, but right now, she didn't care.

Her brothers had long since left, their regular duties on the ranch requiring their attention. Only she and Cash remained, working. Eli had come by and joined them for a short interval, but now he was gone as well and it was just the two of them.

They worked until they ran out of light and then, after Alma had set up several flashlights and lanterns, they worked a little longer.

Until it was steam, not light, that they had run out of.

Cash dropped down on the ground next to her. He leaned back on his elbows and looked up at the sky as it continued to darken.

"Who?" he asked even as he made the logical assumption. "Are you talking about Miss Joan and my grandfather?"

"Yes. I mean, I think your grandfather will be," she elaborated. "He's a darling man and he seems to really love Miss Joan. But my brother did have a point the other night."

Cash thought for a moment, trying to remember what she was referring to. "You mean when he said that he was surprised that Miss Joan said yes?"

"Uh-huh." Eli's comment had made her think. A lot. "Miss Joan has been a fixture here in this town for as long as I can remember, giving out advice and offering support to so many people. She had the sheriff's sister-in-law and her baby living with her until Tina married the doctor. Miss Joan is always doing things like that, and usually not even taking any credit.

"But I think it's kind of strange that a woman who knows everything about everyone else in town never talks about her own past. Nobody knows where she came from before she came to Forever. They don't know if she has any family, or anything. It's like sh only came into existence the moment she walked into town." She slanted a look at him. "Don't you find that a little strange?"

Cash shrugged, trying to remember if he'd ever heard anything that would contradict what Alma had just said. "There've been rumors," he reminded her.

That was her whole point. "But that's just it, there've only been rumors. Nobody knows anything for sure and Miss Joan's certainly not talking about herself. And another thing," she went on. "Miss Joan has had her share of admirers, men who have been interested in her. My dad said that there were even some who asked her to marry them. But Miss Joan always found a reason to back away and turn them down. Why?"

"You tell me."

She sighed, looking back up at the starless sky. "I don't know."

"Maybe she decided she didn't love whoever asked enough—until my grandfather asked." He turned his body toward hers. As he did, he could swear he felt a pull, a strong, insistent pull. He did his best to blame it on his imagination. "Where's this going, Alma?"

"I'm just worried, that's all. I wouldn't want to see your grandfather hurt, he's much too sweet a man."

"He's also a tough old guy," Cash assured her. "He doesn't bruise as easily as you think."

But she didn't agree with him on that. "Even tough old guys can hurt," Alma insisted. "And Harry really loves Miss Joan. I can see it in his eyes every time he looks at her."

Alma was serious, he realized. Her concern amused him. "Tell me, is there anyone in this town you *don't* worry about?"

"You don't have to get sarcastic."

"That's not sarcasm," he told her. "That's a genuine question."

Damn but even in this limited moonlight, hot and sweaty after a full day's work, she looked beautiful to him. *Was* beautiful to him.

And try as he did to ignore it, he could feel the pull between them growing stronger. He had felt it all day, not just when they'd accidentally bumped up against each other, but all day. Just being around her, seeing her, had brought it out.

And now, as Alma lay inches away from him, he could feel the temptation to hold her again, to feel her breathing against him the way he had that last summer, growing progressively more urgent, ensnaring him as it urged him on.

He hadn't thought it was possible to want someone and still be dead inside.

"You can't take care of everyone, Alma," Cash told her quietly.

"No," she agreed, her voice reduced to little more than a whisper. "But I can try."

When had he gotten this close to her? She didn't remember him being this close when he sat down. Now he was less than a full breath away.

She could feel her body, so exhausted only minutes ago, heating in response to his proximity. What was wrong with her? Was she crazy? How could she want something she already knew would end badly? Since when had she become a glutton for punishment?

And yet, how else could she explain it? Because suddenly, all she wanted was one moment back from the past.

Just one moment.

She wanted to feel Cash's lips on hers. Wanted to feel the wild, dizzying surge race throughout her body when he kissed her.

You're asking for trouble, you know that.

If she was, she didn't care.

Just then, a very loud crack of thunder resounded, so close that it felt as if it was rumbling directly beneath them through the ground. Startled, Alma jerked in surprise.

And when she did, she removed the last existing space between them.

Cash's arms closed around her.

The rest of the world receded.

Chapter Nine

The night was warm, but Alma was warmer. She felt like liquid fire in his arms.

At that moment, it occurred to Cash that he could very well have been going against all the forces of nature if he'd attempted to stop what he knew would happen next.

His lips touched hers and it was as if the nomadic journey his soul had been on these past five months had abruptly ended. Without knowing how, or having the benefit of a compass, he'd managed to sail into home port. All the feelings generated by truly coming home rained down on him, filling him.

The light touch of lips suddenly became far more than that.

The kiss deepened, feeding him, making him, however briefly, feel alive again after being so dead inside he'd occasionally take his own pulse just to convince himself that he was still among the living.

As he continued kissing her, Cash gathered her closer still. She lay beneath him on the ground and he tried to absorb whatever healing magic she had in her possession to give. He could feel her heart beating against his, or was that just his, slamming against hers?

Alma's head was spinning even as every fiber in her body rejoiced. She forgot her vow never to allow herself to get close again, to open herself up to the pain destined to follow.

The exhaustion that had consumed her had mysteriously vanished. Every fiber of her body was alert, alive with a strong current of electricity surging through it.

Time and again, his mouth slanted over hers and she threaded her arms around Cash's neck, holding him as close to her as she could, wanting to draw him into her.

To remember when he was gone.

Another crack of thunder all but exploded almost next to them, followed closely by a bolt of lightning that illuminated the sky directly above them. The jarring sound and light show was enough to marginally pull them apart.

"I think maybe we should find some shelter," Cash whispered against her lips.

I already have, Alma thought. Out loud she said, "The barn's close."

So was the house, but someone might come in and find them there, she reasoned, and she wasn't ready to go back to the boundaries that had been there just a few minutes ago. Not yet. Not until they were first completely breached.

"The barn," he echoed in agreement.

Gaining his feet, Cash extended his hand to her to

help her up. Another bolt of lightning streaked across the brow of the sky, turning night into day for less than half a heartbeat.

"Hey!" Gabe called, running toward them from the back porch of the ranch house. "Don't either one of you have enough sense to get out of the rain?"

"It's not raining," Alma pointed out.

"Yet," her brother underscored. "Right now, it's sounding as if it's going to pour at any minute." There was hope in Gabe's voice. The parched land could certainly do with a good soaking. "Besides, that last bolt of lightning looked as if it was only a few yards away from you. I really don't want to have to explain to Dad why his baby girl got electrocuted, so come in, damn it."

"Gabe's right," Cash agreed. "The lightning's too close. We're only inviting trouble, staying out here. We need to get inside, out of harm's way."

Was that how he saw it? she couldn't help wondering, walking in front of him into the house. That kissing her was putting him in harm's way?

She supposed he was right. Had they gone into the barn, things would have escalated and right now, most likely, they'd be making love.

Heaven knew that she certainly had wanted to and if she was *any* judge at all, so had Cash.

The very thought heated her blood.

Alma blew out a breath. She supposed that she

should be grateful to Gabe for unwittingly stopping her from making an awful mistake.

But somehow, she just couldn't muster up even a thimbleful of gratitude.

THE PROMISED STORM NEVER materialized.

Oh, there was a great deal of noise and a few more blinding bolts of lightning, but it was all just a collection of sound and fury, generating nothing.

The rain had moved on to another part of the country. Forever and the surrounding area remained parched and dry.

The county had been the victim of a practical joke played by Mother Nature, Alma thought darkly the next day as she, and the other women who were fortunate to count Miss Joan among their friends, put the finishing touches on almost a dozen different appetizers.

The finished products were arranged along three card tables butted up against one another and covered with one very long tablecloth so as to look like one long table.

A pile of gifts, both store-bought and homemade, graced another table. There were colorful balloons and a two-tiered, intricately decorated cake on yet another table.

All that appeared to be missing was the beloved bride-to-be herself.

Tina, in whom Miss Joan had clearly taken a motherly interest even more so than usual, had been given the job of distracting the not-quite-so-blushing almost-bride and then, at the appropriate time, bringing her back to the house on the pretext that she wanted to show the older woman something.

"Almost time," Olivia announced in what amounted to a stage whisper, signaling that any last-minute preparations had to cease. Miss Joan was liable to appear at any moment and she was the one who had to be taken by surprise, not the other way around.

Full-grown women scurried like children gleefully engaged in a game of tag, taking their places behind furnishings and ducking around corners. Each one of them was to hide and at the appropriate moment jump out and shout "Surprise"—and hope that Miss Joan wouldn't just turn around and walk out. While she loved to interact, Miss Joan decidedly did not like being the center of attention.

Alma, lending Olivia a hand, signaled for the last of the noisy shower guests to silence themselves. If they talked, they wouldn't be able to hear Tina's key in her front door lock.

She managed to convey all this by using a look she'd perfected years ago on her brothers. Silence followed, indicating mission accomplished. Alma smiled to herself.

Miss Joan walked in first. She was in the middle of a lament. "You'd think with all that lightning and thunder, we'd at least get a couple of drops of—"

She stopped talking and abruptly halted as cries of "Surprise!" descended on her from every conceivable angle in the room.

Stunned, she could only stare at the women who were gathered in the family room.

"What's going on?" she asked.

Olivia walked up to her, positioning herself on one side as Tina flanked the other side. Mona, the sheriff's sister, brought up the rear and Alma stood directly in front of her. They were prepared for anything. If Miss Joan was contemplating bolting, she'd find that her escape route was barred on all sides.

"We're throwing you a shower, Miss Joan," Olivia told her.

Miss Joan surprised them all by frowning. "You'd do a lot better if you'd spent your time trying to figure out a way to throw the county a shower."

"Well, given our abilities, this was more in our scope of doable goals," Tina said with a laugh, hugging her.

By definition, Miss Joan was not a hugger, although on occasion she was known to allow herself to be hugged. Because she was so partial to Tina, she stood still for the display of affection although she was clearly not all that comfortable about it.

Miss Joan seemed more uncomfortable to her, Alma thought, than she would have assumed the situation warranted. She began to wonder if there really *was* something wrong, something the rest of them were missing.

"Everyone brought an appetizer," Mona told Miss Joan.

"And presents. There're presents," Tina said with

enthusiasm, indicating the table in the corner that was piled high with gaily wrapped items.

Miss Joan slowly looked at the faces of the women around her. It was impossible to guess what was going through her mind—until she opened her mouth.

She flushed slightly and shook her head. "You shouldn't have done this," she told them, and it seemed to Alma that there was more involved than just a measure of humbleness, surrounding a large dose of self-consciousness.

When had anyone known Miss Joan to be self-conscious—*or* humble?

Something was definitely off.

"It was the least we could do," Alma said, observing the woman carefully. "After all, you were always there for us."

"No," Miss Joan said more firmly, "I mean you *really* shouldn't have done this."

Tina apparently thought modesty was at play here. She put her arm around Miss Joan and gave her a bracing squeeze. "A girl only gets married for the first time once."

That was when Alma saw Miss Joan's face seemingly crumble. Squaring her shoulders, the woman looked as if she was struggling mightily to keep back her tears.

Her voice was tight, and distant, as she begged off. "I'm sorry, but I just can't go through with this." She looked directly at Alma and told her to take her fiancé a message. "Tell Harry that the wedding's off."

And then Miss Joan fled, moving rather quickly for someone who was on her feet for most of the day.

Miss Joan ran out the door. Ran as fast as she could go away from everyone and everything, leaving them to look at one another in mute dismay and absolute confusion.

Alma was the first to recover. "Don't anyone say anything to Harry just yet," she ordered as she went after the older woman.

By the time she got outside, there appeared to be no trace of Miss Joan. But she did run into Cash. Literally. Her body crashed into his.

"What's the hurry?" he asked, grabbing her by the shoulders to steady her.

"Miss Joan just ran out of her own bridal shower. She told me to tell your grandfather that she was sorry, but the wedding was off."

"She what?" He looked at her, stunned. "Why? What happened?"

Alma shrugged helplessly. "It was right after Tina said that a girl only gets married once for the first time. I think she might have gone to the diner—or maybe to her place."

"You stay here, I'll check," he told her.

"But—"

He placed his finger against her lips, silencing her. "Trust me," he told her. "Let me handle this."

Something told her that he needed to. So, although it was against her nature, she forced herself to back off and allow him to handle it.

Alma inclined her head and murmured, "All right, if you think you can talk Miss Joan back into going through with the wedding."

He nodded, not wanting to say anything more right now. He had a couple of ideas to work out in his head as he searched for the woman who was supposed to be marrying his grandfather in less than a week.

Following Alma's instincts, Cash went to the diner first. But although there were a few customers scattered throughout, Miss Joan was nowhere to be seen.

He tried Miss Joan's home next.

Rather than knock, which would have alerted her and given Miss Joan time to bolt if she were so inclined, Cash let himself in—the doors in Forever were never locked during the day—and quietly went from room to room searching for Miss Joan.

When he finally found her a few minutes later, Miss Joan was not in her bedroom but in the tiny family room she hardly ever entered. She was sitting on a hassock, holding what appeared to be a framed photograph against her thin chest and rocking slowly to and fro.

He approached the woman cautiously, taking care not to startle her. "Miss Joan?"

She lifted her head slightly but didn't immediately turn around to look at him. Eyes forward, she stared straight ahead at nothing.

"Go away, Cash," she ordered quietly. "This doesn't concern you."

"Oh, but it does," he contradicted. "You're calling off the wedding. That's going to wind up breaking my grandfather's heart. My grandfather means a great deal to me. I don't want to see him get hurt, so yes, I'd say that this does concern me."

Cash approached the older woman slowly, with measured steps. Half-afraid that she would bolt, he never took his eyes off Miss Joan until he was standing directly in front of her.

"May I see?" he asked, holding out his hand for the photograph.

One moment stretched out into two and then double that again. It looked as if Miss Joan was just going to ignore him. But as he started to ask for a second time to see the photograph, she sighed and surrendered it, frame and all.

Cash glanced down at a faded black-and-white photograph of a handsome young man standing in front of a weathered two-story house. Beside him was a tow-headed little boy. The man was holding the little boy's hand. They both had wide, close to identical, smiles on their faces.

"It was his birthday," Miss Joan said quietly as she continued staring into space. "That picture was taken on Jason's fourth birthday." Her words were addressed to the air that was before her.

"Good-looking little boy," Cash noted. He looked up at Miss Joan. "Who is he?"

"He was my son. The man with him was my husband."

He could hear the pain in her voice each time she uttered the word *was*. He thought of dropping the matter, but that wouldn't solve anything, so he asked, "What happened to them?"

"They died," Miss Joan said with finality, mentally scrambling to gain some high ground, away from the event she was talking about. Away from the piercing pain that the memory always brought with it. "They died and I didn't."

"How?" Cash pressed quietly. His voice was kind.

Miss Joan took in another deep breath, shakier than the one before. Her voice trembled slightly as she answered his question.

"In a tornado. We— I," she corrected since she was the only one left, "lived in Kansas before I came here. The tornado was upon us without warning." She closed her eyes, but she could still see it. Still see it even though it had happened more than four decades ago. "Robert pushed me into the storm cellar and ran to get Jason. I fell off the ladder and broke my leg. I couldn't follow him," she cried, frustration vibrating in every syllable she uttered.

"I heard the wind, heard the house groaning, the beams snapping, but I couldn't do anything. I screamed myself hoarse and eventually I blacked out. When I came to, I started calling again. Some neighbors heard me yelling the next morning and rescued me." The horror of that reality filled her now as if it had just happened. "There was nothing left of my house. Nothing left of my life," she said numbly.

"Two days later they found Robert and Jason miles away, what was left of them," she added quietly, then finally looked up at Cash. "I should have been with them. *Died* with them," she insisted. "It took me a long time to forgive myself for living." Clasping her hands together in her lap, Miss Joan stared down at them. "I just can't open myself up to that kind of pain again, Cash." She shook her head, as if to reinforce her words. "I can't marry your grandfather."

"You're afraid of being happy," he concluded. "Afraid of what it would feel like to have that happiness ripped away from you." He nodded, more sympathetic than the woman could possibly know. "I get that. But in denying yourself, you're also denying my grandfather, who you know loves you a great deal."

A fond smile played on his lips. "You made that man feel young again." And he would always be grateful to her for that. The last time he had seen his grandfather this happy, his grandmother had still been alive. "If he loses you, I'm not sure he'd be able to recover from that. He shouldn't have to lose you," he told her.

"I don't want to hurt him, Cash," Miss Joan protested. "But losing Robert and Jason almost killed me. At my age, if I lost Harry—well, I don't bounce back like I used to," she said philosophically.

"You, Miss Joan, can do anything you set your mind to," he told her with no little admiration. "Besides, these tiny clusters of happiness we're lucky enough to trip over, they're what makes the rest of what we have to put up with bearable."

He knew in his heart that if she did call off the wedding, she would suffer for it as much as his grandfather would.

"Now, I don't know how much longer my grandfather has, or how much longer you have for that matter, but wouldn't it be an awful shame, not to mention a terrible waste, if you allowed yourself—and my grandfather—to be robbed of spending that precious time together just because you're afraid?"

There was that word again, Miss Joan thought. *Afraid.* Yes, there were times when she was afraid, but she wouldn't admit it out loud. Because as long as no one knew, then the fear couldn't own you.

A little bit of her spirit returned as the older woman tossed her head, a few strands of her strawberry-blond hair bouncing against her shoulder as they came loose.

"I'm not afraid," she informed Cash crisply. "I have *never* been afraid. And I'm not about to start being afraid at my age."

He smiled at her. "Atta girl, Miss Joan."

She gave no indication that his words cheered her on. "All right," she announced coolly, "tell your grandfather the wedding's back on."

Cash's eyes crinkled as he said, "I never told him that it wasn't."

"Good," she pronounced. "We don't want to confuse him."

"No," he agreed, "we don't. Besides," he added, doing his best to sound serious, "I'm looking forward to calling you Grandma."

Her eyes narrowed then until they became hazel slits.

"You do, boy, and it's the last thing you'll ever say. To *anyone*."

He laughed at her threat, satisfied that the irrepressible woman was back in form. With a nod he told her, "I'll be sure to keep that in mind."

"See that you do," she instructed. "Now if you'll get out of my way, I have a shower to go back to."

"I'd be honored if you'd let me escort you there," he said, offering her his elbow.

She slipped her hand through it and then looked at him knowingly. "Don't trust me not to change my mind again?" she asked.

"The thought never crossed my mind, Miss Joan," he replied, keeping his expression somber. "I just wanted to be in the company of a fascinating woman for a few extra minutes."

"Liar."

"Nothing that could ever be proven in a court of law," he assured her with a wink.

She shook her head, amused. "You're just like your grandfather."

"I take that as a very high compliment, Miss Joan," he said.

"And well you should, boy," Miss Joan replied.

Chapter Ten

It wasn't until Miss Joan had gone inside and he'd stepped away from the front door of Tina Davenport's home that Cash realized someone was behind him.

Turning around, he saw Alma standing not too far away from him. He had the distinct impression that she hadn't just popped up there within the last minute or two.

Her first words to him confirmed it.

"Nicely done," Alma said, joining him.

Cash moved farther away from Tina's house. He'd initially been on his way to his grandfather's, but he decided to linger just a few minutes longer in town. "You followed me?" he guessed, surprised that she'd do something like that.

Alma didn't bother to lie. There was no point. "Guilty as charged."

He made the only assumption he could. "I take it you didn't trust me to get the job done?"

Alma slowly shook her head, an engaging smile playing on her lips. "On the contrary, I remembered you could be very persuasive when you wanted to be. I just wanted to see how you'd do it."

"So, you approve?" he asked as he raised an eyebrow, waiting for her reply. Had she heard everything? Including Miss Joan sharing her personal tragedy with him?

By watching him break down Miss Joan's defenses and defeating her fears—by the very fact that he had gotten the woman to share with him something she hadn't told anyone else in town—Alma had been stirred to a near melting point. Listening to him, she'd found, had played on her empathy, not to mention her feelings of pride in the man Cash was, as well as awakening a host of other feelings.

To explain her reaction to what he'd done for Miss Joan seemed next to impossible. But to show him, well, she definitely could do that, and she knew for a fact that there were times when actions spoke louder than words.

So, as he watched her, Alma moved in closer to him, took his face between her hands and, standing on her very tiptoes, she pressed her lips against his.

The moment she did, it was as if some sort of inner explosion of massive proportions occurred. An inner explosion that immediately and completely encompassed both of them.

But after that moment of absolutely pure pleasure, it was Cash who pulled away, mindful of the gathering taking place just a few yards away.

He didn't want Alma to become the subject of any gossip on his account.

As he took a breath, he could feel his heart racing madly. "You keep doing that and I might not be able to walk away next time."

She looked at him for a long moment, trying to discern what was on his mind. She couldn't, so she went with instincts instead. "Who said anything about walking away?"

Damn it, if he remained around her, talking like this, he was liable to kiss her again. And not to stop there.

"Don't you have a shower to attend?" he asked, nodding toward the house.

She glanced over her shoulder for just a second. "Miss Joan'll keep them all busy. They won't even notice I'm not there." She shrugged dismissively. "I can always say an emergency called me away."

"Like what? A squirrel falling out of a tree?"

"You can never be too careful with those falling squirrels," she deadpanned, looking very solemn. "It might bite if it lands on your shoulder."

Amused, he played along, even though he knew he shouldn't, for her sake. "Wouldn't want that."

"Nope," she agreed, turning up her face to his, a silent invitation. "You certainly wouldn't."

Unable to resist any longer, he lowered his mouth to hers and kissed her again.

This time, she cleaved to him because she knew deep down that he was the part of her that had been missing all this time. Alma continued to press against him as she felt her body heating to a degree that could have melted a pat of butter within three feet of her.

Again Cash drew away, although this time it took him a great deal more effort than it had just a moment ago. But he couldn't allow her to do this to herself.

He wasn't any good for her.

"Oh, damn it, Alma, you don't want this." He was damaged inside, too damaged to deserve someone like her. "I'm not the person you remember."

Her pulse was racing and everything inside her felt truly alive again. She wasn't going to allow Cash to run himself down like this.

"Yes, you are," she told him quietly, firmly. "You are exactly as I remember you."

She was convinced now that while Cash had initially been mesmerized by what a city like Los Angeles had to offer, mesmerized by the fast pace and the sophistication he'd encountered, that something else had broken him to this degree.

Which, in turn, meant that he wasn't completely responsible for having stayed away so long.

And even if he was, she knew that she forgave him. Forgave the man who was, because of the man he had once been. A man she had loved utterly and completely. That wasn't something a person easily walked away from.

Her eyes met his. "Take me to my place," she whispered.

Five very simple words. And yet, she couldn't have been more seductive if she'd tried.

He would have found a way somehow to step away

if Alma had changed her mind. But he would have been lying to himself if he didn't admit that he would have been twice as wounded by her unspoken rejection as he'd been at the outset.

It was a moot point.

Alma's sultry invitation made it impossible for him to hold her at arm's length any longer.

"Your place," he echoed.

She took him by the hand, leading him to his car. It was the closer of the two.

"I'll give you directions as we go," she promised.

He had no doubt that she would.

CASH WAS NOT SURE HOW HE managed to drive the short distance from Tina's home to Alma's small one-story house. He really had no memory of it. One moment he was getting into his car, the next she was telling him to pull up in front of "that one."

The only thing he clearly remembered was Alma. Alma, sitting beside him, looking like sunshine, smelling like sin.

He was vaguely aware of getting out of the car, acutely aware of the ache in his gut, the ache from wanting her.

The second they were inside her home, the frenzy began, not to be denied any longer.

He sealed his mouth to hers, and the impact of their coming together was so hard that Alma slammed her back against the door, closing it.

She had the presence of mind—what there was left of it—to reach behind her and turn the bolt, locking the door. She wanted no one walking in on them, not by accident or design.

She wanted him all to herself.

The second the door was locked, the desire vibrating within her leaped up another five notches. Like a woman possessed, Alma began to pull at his clothes.

Her movements became more frantic with each item she attacked and managed to remove. One of his buttons went flying across the room in protest.

Before he could take note of it or say anything, she said, "I sew," against his mouth.

She tasted his brief chuckle before it faded away.

Spurred on by her, his blood heating fast, he found that his hands couldn't remain idle. He began to remove her clothes one piece at a time.

Although the same urgency roared through his veins as did through hers, Cash was careful to rein himself in. Otherwise, all her clothes would have been scattered about the room, limp and in tatters.

As it was, they were still scattered, but he didn't have her unclothed as quickly as he would have wanted to. He was determined to exhibit some restraint.

He wanted this to last awhile.

And when she was finally naked, Cash dropped to his knees, anointing every inch of her with hot lips and kisses that drove her up and over to her first climax.

They'd been inside the house for less than seven minutes.

Rather than having her desire sated, Alma only felt it ratcheted up to a higher plateau.

Alma dropped down to her own knees, resealing her mouth to his, kissing him back so hard that they both wound up on the floor, their bodies as utterly entwined as their mouths.

Time temporarily ceased to exist. There was no before, no after. No past, no future. There was only now and it was encased in a bubble around the two of them.

For her, their lovemaking had the feel of familiarity to it, and yet, it was all brand-new.

Different, but the same.

Unable to explore and understand, Alma simply gloried in what was, absorbing each sensation, each feeling as it burst over her. Loving the fact that she had this one more time with the only man she had ever loved.

Perhaps another woman would have held out, would have used the hurt she'd sustained when he had so abruptly dropped out of her life and held it up as a shield. But another woman hadn't loved so utterly, so completely as she had.

As she did.

She tried very hard not to have illusions that this was just the beginning of the rest of their lives together. Alma knew better.

It was what it was: glorious.

Beyond that, she would be a fool to have any further expectations.

He'd missed her. Oh, God, how he had missed her.

He hadn't realized until this moment the true depth of just how much. Sleepwalking through his life for the past five months, suddenly it was as if he were whole again.

Cash knew it wasn't possible, and yet, there it was. She was the other half of him and he should have acknowledged that, realized that, so very long ago.

Now, it was too late.

He had nothing to offer her, nothing to make her stay. He was no longer the boy with dreams; he was the man with ashes where his soul had once been.

And, if he were truly decent, he wouldn't have given in to himself this way, wouldn't have acted on his urges. No matter what it cost him, he should have walked away from her as quickly as possible, before any of this had gotten out of hand.

But he wasn't decent. It was as if the memory of his soul had begged him for just one more time, one more taste of heaven with her.

A man could only be so strong and he was beyond able to turn away on his own.

Cash ran his hands along the length of her.

He did the same with his lips.

For just a precious moment, he claimed Alma one more time as his very own, knowing full well that he had no right to.

Moving into position over her, he saw himself reflected in her eyes and for just that tiny second, Cash felt redeemed. Felt like the person he had once been—

whole and hopeful—before the world had come crashing down on him.

Through his own fault.

He shut the thought away. He wanted this moment with Alma. *Needed* this moment with Alma.

Their fingers intertwined, Cash slowly entered her. The look in her eyes nearly drove him wild. He felt Alma raise her hips to seal the union. When she moved beneath him, the rhythm of the dance, *their* dance, began.

And when it did, there was nothing else, just the two of them as they moved faster and faster, racing together to journey's end.

It arrived much too quickly, enfolding both of them in its embrace, holding them tightly in its grip. Just for a wondrous megasecond, they found themselves suspended in time and space.

The fall came, as it always did, bringing them back to earth.

Cash held on to her even more tightly than before, not wanting their precious time together to end. Not wanting his sanity to return, dragging reality and his ever-present remorse in its wake.

Cash remained where he was, holding her in his arms, waiting for his breathing to return to normal. He pressed a kiss to the top of her head, thinking how precious Alma was to him. How he'd been a blind fool to lose sight of that and go after things that only represented material gain.

That sort of wealth was useless in the real scheme of things.

"I'm sorry, Alma," Cash whispered.

His voice was barely audible, but she'd heard him, heard the words that rippled along her skin. For a second, something quickened within her, bracing her. Making her feel ill.

She banked down the feeling.

He wasn't saying what she thought, she told herself. He *wasn't*.

"I'm not going to ask for what," she told him softly. "I'm just going to tell you that it's all right. Whatever you're sorry for, it's all right."

"No," he told her, his voice quiet but firm nonetheless. "It's not."

Shifting, Alma raised herself up on her elbow to look at him. She could tell by the expression on his face that he wasn't about to talk about what was eating away at him so completely. Not yet. He wasn't ready and she could understand that, even though it troubled her to see him suffering like this. Because, no matter what he pretended and how hard he worked at putting up a front, he *was* suffering.

But there was one thing she could say to him, no matter what it turned out to be.

"You've got to forgive yourself, Cash."

Didn't she think he would if he could? But this wasn't some minor infraction. This transgression had permanent consequences attached to it. And the mistake had been his.

"This isn't forgivable," he told her.

There they had a major difference of opinion. "*Everything* is forgivable," she answered with conviction. "Besides, you're not capable of doing something so awful that there's no forgiving you."

The laugh was harsh and self-deprecating. "You don't know me."

Is that what he thought? How could he? She knew him, her *soul* knew him.

Alma touched his face. "You're wrong. I *do* know you, know the person you were and still are," she told him, lightly pointing to his chest with her index finger. "You might have gotten a little lost for a while, but underneath it all, you're still the guy who would get up super early to help his grandfather out with chores before he went off to school."

Cash shook his head. He'd give anything to go back, to be that kid again and this time stay on course, follow his convictions, not the money. "He died a long time ago, Alma."

She put her finger to his lips. "Shh. I won't have you talking badly about my best friend like that. About the guy who lit up my world then."

There was no point in wishing for it to happen. It wasn't going to. He was this monster who had fought to set a murderer free and succeeded because of a technicality.

Succeeded.

The word had an incredibly hollow ring to it.

"But—"

She sighed and shook her head. "I guess there's just one way to deal with you, Taylor. Just one proven way to keep you quiet."

He loved the smile in her eyes. Loved the way she looked at him with affection even though he knew he didn't deserve it.

"Alma—"

She pushed him back down with the flat of her hand, agilely moving over him until she'd straddled his body. Alma leaned over him, the tips of her hair lightly brushing against his bare skin, causing him to react. To want her all over again.

A wicked smile spread over her lips. She could feel him hardening.

"Ah, it appears you might be ready for some more persuasive dialogue."

He wasn't sure how she did it, but somehow, she managed to drain the sadness from him again. She'd bought him a little more time in which to feel human.

Cash threaded his hands through her hair, bringing her closer to him. "You'd be hell on wheels in a courtroom, you know that?"

Alma grinned then. He was the lawyer, not her. But that didn't mean that she couldn't carry on one hell of an argument if she wanted to.

"We all do what we can," she told him. Then her expression grew more solemn as she brought her mouth to within inches of his. "It's a dirty job," she told him just before she kissed him again, "but, hey, someone's got to do it."

After that, he forgot to try to push her away, forgot to be noble for her sake.

Forgot everything except how happy he felt when he made love with her.

Chapter Eleven

As far back as she could remember, Alma had always been a unique kind of light sleeper. If a noise was something she had come to expect and was used to, she could sleep right through it. If she fell asleep during a thunderstorm, then a particularly loud crack of thunder wouldn't wake her and she'd sleep right through it.

But any sort of noise that was out of place, any movement her subconscious couldn't account for, and she would instantly be awake.

So when she felt the bed shifting ever so slightly because of a weight change, felt the warmth of Cash's body withdrawing from her, Alma opened her eyes because her senses had alerted her that *something* was different.

And then she realized what.

Cash was getting up. Leaving.

She turned her head ever so slowly and saw that he was sitting up on the edge of the bed with his back to her. The set of his shoulders, even in a room that was predominantly dark except for the subtle rays of moonlight peeking in, told her that he was getting ready to go.

For a second she debated pretending she was still asleep, allowing him his getaway. The next moment she thought it might be the wrong approach. Maybe Cash was constantly evading his problem—whatever it was—rather than facing it head-on. Ducking it rather than tackling it until it just dissipated.

Silence, in this case, she decided, was *not* golden. "So, same time, same place, ten years from now?" she asked him.

The sound of her voice startled Cash. He turned around to look at her, as if to confirm what he already knew. "You're awake."

"Either that, or I'm exceedingly coherent when I talk in my sleep," she quipped. Tucking the sheet around her breasts, Alma sat up. "Didn't anyone ever teach you that it's bad manners to just sneak off in the middle of the night after making wild, passionate love to a woman and reducing her to a puddle of mush?"

He laughed at the imagery. If anyone had melted last night, it had been him. "You weren't reduced to a puddle of mush."

"Well, it was close," she allowed. "But that's not the point. The point is you're not supposed to leave in the dead of night like some thief, although," she reconsidered, "I suppose in a way, you are."

Though there was a smile on her lips, she was deadly serious with her analogy. She didn't have to tell him that he'd stolen her heart all over again. He knew.

How could he not?

Cash shook his head. It would take so little for him to give in and stay until morning. Stay and wake up to the scent, to the comforting and arousing feel of her. But he had to stop indulging himself. He had to think of her. He cared about her too much to pull her into his dark world.

"Like a thief or not, it's best for you if I do leave," he assured her.

Tossing her head, Alma scrambled up to her knees, a regal princess whose vestments repeatedly fell away unless she was vigilant. She fussed with the sheet one more time, then gave up. Modesty was not the issue here.

The note of playfulness was missing from her voice as she told him, "In case you haven't noticed, Counselor, I'm a big girl now and I'm the one who gets to decide what's best for me. That's really not up to you or to anyone else."

The moonlight was on her face. There was a flash in her eyes as she made her declaration. He'd forgotten how very feisty she could get when she felt she was being marginalized or ignored. There was something magnificent and spellbinding about the sight. The fact that she sat before him, nude, only underscored his reaction.

"For the record, Alma, I noticed. I noticed," he repeated with feeling. "But that still doesn't change anything. What I said last night was—and is—true. I'm not any good for you." He looked off into the darkness. "I'm not any good for anyone."

"I'm sorry, but you're wrong," she informed him. "You're good for Miss Joan and for your grandfather. You talked her out of calling off the wedding and possibly ruining not just the rest of your grandfather's life, but her own, as well." She smiled at him. "Everyone knows they belong together."

Just like you and I belong together, you big, dumb idiot.

"If you hadn't talked to her the way you did," she continued, "if you hadn't gotten her to open up like that, your grandfather would be nursing a broken heart right now and who knows, Miss Joan might have gotten so embarrassed by practically leaving him at the altar that she might have decided to pack up after all these years and move on."

She looked at him pointedly. "You saved two lives from being ruined and who knows how many other lives were actually affected by what you did?" she posed. Alma leaned over, covering his hand with her own. "A lot of people look to Miss Joan to help them with their relationships. They would have no one to turn to if she was gone. You did a lot of good yesterday."

The bond Alma was creating just by touching his hand felt very intimate. She made it difficult for him to think, to hold on to his resolve. And having her nude like this wasn't exactly helping him, either. He was fighting a very real urge to make love with her again.

"And apparently, your imagination knows no bounds," he told her.

Her eyes danced as they slid over his nude body. Her pulse went into double time. "You don't know the half of it. But I am willing to put your assumption to the test," she said mischievously.

What was it about being around this woman that helped him forget his demons? He knew he was being selfish, but it was such a relief to put his burden down, even for a few moments.

"What are you getting at?" he asked.

She patted the mattress in front of her. "Come back to bed and I'll show you."

"I guess it's probably too late to make my covert escape," Cash relented.

The middle of the night seemed to be the loneliest time by far and if there was a way to temporarily stave off that dark, empty feeling, then he was all for it. At least for now.

She let her sheet pool about her thighs as she threaded her arms around his neck. Shifting, she drew closer to him.

He could feel himself wanting her all over again. Wanting her as if he hadn't already been with her three times since he'd brought her home yesterday.

Again he wondered just what kind of power she had over him, and why couldn't he get himself under control? Why couldn't he do what he knew was right instead of indulging himself this way?

"This doesn't change anything," he told her with

effort as he felt her press her lips to the side of his neck. The pit of his stomach instantly quickened the moment he felt her skin against his, even as other parts of his body were reacting accordingly.

"I know," she answered breathlessly, as enthralled as he was. "Don't worry, we can take this one baby step at a time."

Somewhere in the middle of the night, she'd realized that Cash *did* want, as well as need, forever. He was just afraid to admit it to himself and especially afraid to admit it to anyone else. But she was going to help him with that, no matter how long it took. And if that involved baby steps, so be it.

Alma drew back just enough to create a little space between them. Space enough for Cash to be able to look at her. She could see the desire in his eyes and it pulled at her. She spread her arms out to him.

"You can take your first baby step now if you'd like," she coaxed.

As if he could actually turn away. "Damn but you are hard to resist."

She smiled serenely as she closed her arms around his neck and pressed her body against his again. "That, dear sir, is the whole idea."

The sound of his laughter filled her heart as well as her bedroom and he forgot all about leaving. Just as she'd hoped.

"WHAT HAPPENED TO YOU Saturday?" Rick asked the following Monday morning. It was early and just the two of them for now. He found her by the coffeemaker, filling her mug. Alma raised an eyebrow in response to his question. "Olivia said you seemed to disappear about the same time that Miss Joan did, except that when she came back, you didn't."

Alma avoided his eyes as she said, "I had something to take care of."

Rick smiled knowingly. "How's he doing?" He followed her back to her desk and, nursing his second mug of coffee of the morning, he leaned against her desk. "And don't insult my intelligence by asking who."

"Wouldn't dream of it." She knew better than to play games with Rick. He was her friend as well as her boss and she had a great deal of respect for him. "I think that he's got something fighting him for his soul," she told Rick honestly, then hazarded a guess. "I've got a feeling that something happened to him when he was out there in Los Angeles, something that he can't get over or forgive himself for."

Rick mulled over her words. "You have any idea what?"

Feeling helpless, Alma shook her head. "No, and I'd give anything to know. As close as I can figure it out, it has something to do with his being a lawyer. When I called his firm when he first got here, they told me that Cash was on a leave of absence." She looked at Rick over her mug. "Not a vacation," she underscored, "but a leave of absence. That tells me that he doesn't know if he's planning on going back to Los Angeles or not."

And as much as she wanted Cash to stay in Forever,

it had to be for the right reasons, not because he was running from something. He wouldn't be able to respect himself if that was why he was here.

Rick shrugged. "Maybe he wants to stay here."

If only it was that black-and-white. "I don't think it's so much a case of his wanting to be somewhere as his *not* wanting to be in Los Angeles."

Rick read between the lines to get at the heart of what she was saying. "You think he's running from something?"

"You mean like something he did?" She honestly didn't know, but she hoped not. "I'm not sure, but there are times when I think that it's himself Cash is trying to ditch."

Rick laughed shortly. "Not exactly something that's easily done."

"No," she agreed, then, with a quiet sigh, Alma amended her initial answer. "At least not in the usual sense."

"You mean you think he might try to kill himself?"

Alma pressed her lips together as she continued holding the coffee mug between her hands. She could feel that it was getting cold, but hot coffee wasn't the issue here. She wanted to unravel the puzzle that Cash Taylor had become.

She stared off into space, trying to pull her thoughts together. Trying to make sense of it all. When had life gotten so complicated? Forever was a simple, uncomplicated little town.

Or had been.

"I honestly don't know." And then she looked up at Rick. "But I'm going to do everything I can to keep Cash from doing anything really stupid."

Which was as close as she would come to saying that Cash was capable of ending his life. But she'd seen the flicker of desperation in his eyes when he didn't know she was looking. Seen the sadness, the vast emptiness that seemed at times to threaten to swallow him up. And *that* frightened her.

Rick nodded in response to her last words. "Let me know if you need any backup," Rick said simply.

Alma nodded. "Thanks." It went without saying that she could always count on him and she was grateful for that. "By the way, how's the little one?" she asked. "I haven't seen a new picture in, oh, at least two days. What happened? You get tired of taking them?" she teased, knowing full well that the sheriff felt he and his wife had the most beautiful little girl in the entire world and never hesitated to produce the photographs to prove it. So far, they seemed to be intent on visually documenting every day of their daughter's very short life.

"As a matter of fact, I've got a few new ones to show you," Rick said. "They're on my desk in the office. I'll go get them." And then he paused to look at her over his shoulder. "That'll teach you to ask."

Alma's eyes were smiling as she said, "I guess it will."

SHE'D HOPED THAT CASH would either call her or just come around, but he did neither. Alma did her best to take it in stride, but despite her endless, silent pep talks, she would have been lying to herself if she pretended that it didn't bother her.

It did. A lot.

Well, what did you expect? To have him suddenly transformed by the power of your love like in some Hollywood movie? The man has issues, there's something eating away at him. For all you know, it might have to do with a woman he was dating. Maybe they broke it off and she took her own life, so he feels guilty. Or maybe he let her slip away and now he really feels that he lost a good thing. You just don't know.

She didn't, and it was driving her crazy despite promises to herself to leave it alone. About the only thing she could be certain of was that the Cash she knew wouldn't have been berating himself this way over some minor infraction.

But what?

What had he done?

She couldn't help him if she didn't know and he wouldn't tell her.

Maybe Miss Joan knew. Maybe, because the woman had shared her innermost secret with him, Cash had turned around and confessed to her.

She hadn't seen Miss Joan since the beginning of her bridal shower three days ago. She hadn't gone by the diner for her ritual first cup of coffee of the morning for a couple of days.

On the fourth morning, Alma decided that it might not be such a bad idea to drop by the diner. At seven it wouldn't be too crowded yet and she'd get a chance to have a couple of words with Miss Joan without having to worry about ten other people overhearing them.

When she walked into the diner, she saw Miss Joan, as usual, standing behind the counter. Seeing the older woman was one of those comforting things, one of the things in life she could count on.

It made her smile.

Miss Joan looked her way. "Hello, stranger. I thought maybe you'd decided to swear off the diner." Miss Joan inclined her head in a greeting. "Nice to see you again."

Well, there was no time like the present to get the apology/excuse out of the way. She cleared her throat. "About your shower—"

Miss Joan held up her hand like a patrolman directing traffic, abruptly halting the flow of words. "If you're going to give me some lame excuse about why you weren't there for the second half, don't bother. Besides, you bought yourself a lot of leeway."

Alma didn't follow. "I did?"

"Don't act dumb, it doesn't become you."

"I'm not acting," Alma protested.

"Even worse," Miss Joan said, shaking her head. And then a half smile creased her thin lips. "The way I see it, you put Cash up to going after me." It was clear that she wasn't about to believe any other explanation. "Best shower gift you could have given me," Miss Joan declared unabashedly. "Because he kept after me, I got something off my chest that's been bothering me for a real long time. After I got it out, I had the feeling that

I was getting a second shot at things—a second shot at happiness—thanks to Cash."

Alma wondered what the woman would say if she knew that she'd overheard her confession, that she knew all about the tragedy that haunted the woman. That was best left unsaid. But something else wasn't. Cash had lowered his voice for a couple of minutes at one point, speaking so softly that she wasn't able to hear him. Had he confessed something to Miss Joan, to make it seem like more of an equal exchange?

"Did he happen to get anything off *his* chest?" she asked hopefully.

Miss Joan knew exactly what she was asking about. "You mean like what's been bothering him? Why he came back here when he did?"

"Well, he came back for the wedding," Alma pointed out. "But—"

Miss Joan stopped her with a shake of her head. "That was just the excuse that got him here. But he would have come back here one way or another. After all, this is where his roots are, where he had his dreams." Miss Joan paused and looked at her significantly. "And where his best friend still is."

She thought of her brothers and how they and Cash used to hang out together—and how much useless energy they had spent, trying to ditch her. "Are you talking about Gabe or Eli?"

"I'm talking about you, little Miss Innocent," Miss Joan informed her. "If you ask me, Cash came back here to start over—he just might not know it yet," she allowed. "But that's why he came." Clearing off the counter from the last customer, she deposited the dishes onto a tray and placed it on the counter where the cook would put completed orders. "If you're interested, Cash is working at your dad's place, hustling to get that flowered thing he's working on ready in time for the wedding."

Alma's mouth dropped open in surprise. She thought for sure that just this once, Miss Joan and Harry had been kept in the dark. "Miss Joan," she cried, distressed. "You're not supposed to—"

"Know about it?" Miss Joan completed the young woman's protest with a laugh. "Honey," she said, coming closer so that she could lean over the counter. "I know about everything." But then she paused. "Well, almost everything," she amended, then pinned Alma down with a look. "The point is, why don't you go out there and see if he needs a hand—or a shoulder?"

He'd had plenty of opportunity to lean on her and hadn't. Turning up by his side with a hammer wouldn't spark a soul-cleansing confession. She didn't want to seem as if she was throwing herself at him. "He knows where to find me."

"And you know where to find him," Miss Joan said impatiently. "And so you two are going to do what? Hide behind some made-up excuses, waiting for the other to relent? Honey, that's how wars get started, not stories with happy endings. Tell that sheriff of ours you're taking some time off and go to Cash." Her eyes narrowed down to small slits. "Just because he doesn't say so doesn't mean he doesn't need you."

Miss Joan was right, Alma thought, relenting.

So what else was new?

"Okay." Halfway to the door, Alma turned around and called out, "Miss Joan?"

Miss Joan turned to glance at her over her shoulder. "Yeah?"

"Nice to have you back."

Miss Joan nodded, not bothering to contradict the young woman. "Nice to be back," she said just as Alma hurried out the door.

Chapter Twelve

She could have driven there blindfolded if she had to.

The road to her father's ranch from town was completely embossed on Alma's brain. But in deference to the many wildlife creatures that lived in and around the area and could bolt right in front of her vehicle at any given, unexpected moment, she watched the road intently.

Approaching the ranch, Alma listened for the sound of hammering or sawing, but she didn't hear either one. Instead, she heard the sound of raised voices. Coming to a stop before the ranch house, she got out of the car and immediately recognized Cash's voice.

But the other voice didn't belong to anyone in her family.

It was only belatedly that she realized the other person involved in what was apparently an argument was Cash's grandfather. So much for the arch being a surprise for either the bride or the groom, because obviously Harry hadn't been kept in the dark about what was going on, either. But that wouldn't have prompted his shouting at Cash and there definitely was shouting.

What the hell was going on? she wondered, quickening her pace.

Alma hurried around the perimeter of the house and made her way toward the barn. Her brothers were nowhere to be seen and it seemed that no one was working on the seven-foot-tall wedding gift.

Standing in front of it were Cash, his grandfather and her father, Miguel. The latter attempted to defuse what threatened to become an explosive situation at any moment, and he wasn't having any luck. Neither side paid any attention to him.

"Hey, what's going on here?" Alma asked, raising her voice so that it all but drowned out the sound of the other two voices.

The element of surprise was on her side and for a split second the two men stopped trying to outshout each other as both turned to look at her.

Looking just a little like one of the prophets straight out of biblical times, thanks to his full head of silvery gray hair that came an inch shy of dipping down to his shoulders, Cash's grandfather frowned at her abrupt intrusion.

"No disrespect, Alma," he told her, "but this doesn't concern you."

"Maybe not," she allowed, casually hooking her thumbs just above her gun belt, "but keeping the peace does and you two are disturbing it."

Clearly frustrated, both by his grandfather's attitude and by her sudden appearance in the midst of the argument, Cash narrowed his eyes as he looked in her direction.

"Who filed a complaint?" he asked. "The horses?"

Alma pretended that he hadn't said anything. She was not about to get sidetracked into an exchange of words with him.

Shooting Cash a look that would have cut down a lesser man, she said, "We need to talk later," then turned her attention back to the immediate situation. "Now, why are the two of you shouting at each other?"

"We weren't shouting," Harry protested. "He's just too stubborn to listen so I had to raise my voice a little to make him hear."

"*I'm* the stubborn one?" Cash cried incredulously. "Isn't that a lot like the damn pot calling the kettle black?"

Alma held up her hand to silence him, but when that didn't curtail either of the raised voices, she let loose with an ear-piercing whistle. *That* brought the two men to a grinding halt.

"That's better," she pronounced with approval when they both were struck silent. "Now, let's put away the aforementioned kitchenware and one of you tell me what seems to be the problem." Because she was still trying to work through a fresh batch of hurt feelings, courtesy of Cash, she turned toward his grandfather. "Harry?"

"The problem is Cash just won't listen," Harry accused.

"The problem is he's too full of pride," Cash complained at the same time, their voices blending to produce one nearly unintelligible answer.

It took Alma a minute to separate the two sentences and make sense out of what the men were saying. She turned toward her father for help. "Dad, can you possibly shed a little light on what they're talking about?"

Her father lifted his broad shoulders in a helpless shrug. "I would if I could, Alma, but I came out when I heard them arguing."

"It's not arguing," Harry insisted firmly. "I'm just trying to talk some sense into this stubborn mule." He gestured disparagingly at his grandson.

"Funny," Cash countered pointedly, "I was just about to say the same thing about you."

"What is this all about?" Alma asked again, enunciating each word slowly, deliberately. And then she pointed to Cash's grandfather. "You first, Harry."

Harry tossed his head, his mane regally flying over his shoulder. "I told him I didn't need his charity."

Cash broke into the narrative. "It's not charity," he insisted angrily.

"*What's* not charity?" Alma asked before the argument could escalate again.

"He went and paid off my note on the ranch," Harry accused, saying it the way he would have if he were reporting the commission of a crime to the proper authorities.

Alma blinked, surprised. "You had a note on the ranch?" she asked. "I thought you paid off the mortgage a long time ago."

"I did, but times got a little rough and I needed a loan to tide me over," he murmured, his voice dropping as he looked away.

"He took out a note to pay for my college education. *Then* the economy went bad and he started losing money, so he couldn't meet the loan payments," Cash said, jumping into the narrative. "All of which he kept from me. If I hadn't seen the notice-of-foreclosure letter on his desk—"

"Which you had no business reading," Harry protested angrily. "He snuck off and paid the note on the house behind my back!" the older man said indignantly.

The situation had a definite déjà vu flavor about it, reminding Alma of the way she and her brothers had pitched in to help pay off all their mother's medical bills.

"Harry," Alma interjected kindly, "family *always* has the right to butt in. That's what makes them better people. You rely on each other. That's what makes you family."

"I don't want charity," Harry declared again stubbornly. Scowling, he crossed his arms before him, looking every inch like the Norse god of war.

Very deftly, Alma turned the tables on him. "Was it charity when you took Cash and his mother in after his dad was killed in that offshore drilling rig accident?" she asked the older man.

The very question offended Harry. "Of course not," he said indignantly, "but that was different."

"No, it wasn't," she pointed out patiently. "They

needed you and you were there, opening your doors and taking them in. You gave them a home, Harry. There is no price tag on that, and Cash just wants to try to return some of the favor. And he can do that by *saving* your home—and his," she reminded the rancher. "It is his home, you know. You told him that your home would always be his home as well, remember?"

Reaching, she put her hand on the man's shoulder. "The polite thing to do is just accept the favor in the spirit it was tendered. If it helps you any, think of it as a wedding present," she suggested.

"Cash has already given me—us—a wedding present," Harry protested. "A mighty generous one. He gave us two first-class plane tickets to Hawaii and he's paying for a two-week stay in this really fancy hotel. I can't accept both," he declared. "That wouldn't be right."

Out of the corner of her eye, Alma saw Cash opening his mouth to launch into a rebuttal. She held up her hand for him to hold his peace as she addressed his grandfather's concerns.

"Sure you can," she told Harry. "It's the gracious thing to do. It makes Cash happy to do this for you, for both of you. Don't you want your grandson to be happy, Harry?"

Harry felt as if the road had somehow twisted in another direction beneath his feet. "Well, yeah, sure I do, but—"

"All right, then it's settled," Alma declared, cutting in before Harry could launch into phase two of his argument. "You're going on a two-week honeymoon with your bride and when you come back you'll have a ranch to come home to. What could be better?"

"Well, when you put it that way..." Harry attempted to appear disgruntled one more time, but it was only an act. Blowing out a long, heartfelt sigh, Harry glanced at Alma's father, his lifelong friend, and asked, "You ever win an argument with her, Mike?"

Miguel Rodriguez shook his head and laughed. "Not since she was four. None of us in the family have," he added.

Harry nodded, as if he hadn't expected anything else. "I didn't think so." And then he regarded his grandson. "Thank you, boy," he said with feeling. "But I still say this is too generous."

"Don't worry, he can afford it," Alma assured the man. She'd heard a great deal about the firm Cash worked for and how elite they were considered. Some of the clients they took on were rich beyond the average person's dreams. "Besides, it's what he wants to do. So hug, make up and let the man get back to working on your surprise wedding arch."

Turning to look at the almost-completed structure— it still needed to have flowers woven through it—she felt obliged to ask, "Does *anyone* not know about this?"

Miguel answered for his friend. "No, I think it's pretty safe to say that everyone in Forever knows about it."

Alma pressed her lips together as she appraised the arch. "Well, at least you won't have to try to transport it in the middle of the night in order to keep it a surprise," she said philosophically. "That's one worry down."

"What did I tell you?" Miguel said to Cash. "She *always* finds the silver lining to everything—even if it looks hopeless."

Harry nodded, getting on the other side of his grandson. "If you ask me, that's a really good quality to have."

"Speaking of asking," Miguel said, picking up on the word, "I've got a pot of coffee on the stove." He looked at Harry. "You up for a cup?"

"If you're playing host," Harry told him, "I'd just as soon have a cold beer."

Miguel grinned, the laugh lines about his eyes crinkling. "Even better. Let's go inside, it's hot out here."

Alma turned to Cash as her father and his grandfather disappeared into the house. "He's right, you know. It *is* hot out here. Maybe you should go inside now, wait until it's cooler to finish working on that."

"Heat doesn't bother me," he told her. He took a step up the ladder, then paused. "Besides, I've forgotten how much I enjoy working with my hands." He gazed down at her for a long moment, then lowered his voice before saying, "Forgot how much I liked being with you, too."

Was that his way of apologizing again? Or did he think she hadn't even noticed? Or was she so wrapped up in whatever it was that was bothering him that he couldn't even see outside his glass prison?

For now, because she'd just quelled one potential flare-up, she decided to keep the situation light. "Is that why you disappeared for two days? You don't phone, you don't write—"

But he didn't banter back. Cash was dead serious when he told her in response, "That was for your own good, not mine."

Alma watched him climb up the rest of the way on the ladder so he could finish working on the top of the arch. "I thought we settled that line of thinking Sunday morning. Remember?" she prodded. "I said I could decide for myself what was and wasn't good for me?"

He looked as if he was just going to let that go, but then he couldn't. "Not if you don't know the whole story," he pointed out.

She stood below him at the base of the ladder, her hands on either side to keep it steady. "Then tell me the whole story," she pleaded.

The need to unburden himself was tremendous, but at what cost? he asked himself. If he told her everything and she was repelled by what he'd done, how could he cope? How could he see her looking at him differently and still be able to go on?

No, it was better just to keep it to himself, to pretend that she wouldn't judge him and that eventually things would somehow work themselves out. That eventually, his guilt would lessen and that he would learn how to live with what he'd done.

He shook his head in response to her entreaty. "I can't, Alma. Not yet." And then, because he had to be honest with her, since she deserved nothing less, he said, "Maybe not ever."

It was like being slapped in the face. He was supposed to trust her, to know that no matter what, she would be on his side.

"I can't accept that." But to keep from having this escalate and get out of hand, she made him a counteroffer. "But I'm willing to put up with 'not yet' for a little while."

He laughed, shaking his head. "I forgot how you could argue the birds out of the trees."

She grinned. "Funny, I never thought of you as being a bird, but, hey—" she shrugged "—whatever works."

"Speaking of 'works,' I'd better get back to working or this thing is never going to be ready on time for the wedding."

No matter what, he still kept his word, she thought. Which meant that there *was* hope for him. "You do realize that my brothers left you to do most of the work here, right?"

"I don't mind." He paused to hammer in another nail to secure the arch. "They've got work to do. I'm just here on vacation."

Well, that certainly didn't ring true, Alma thought with a sudden pang. But she wasn't about to call him out on it, not yet. Instead, she pretended that she didn't know he'd taken a leave of absence from his firm. "So you're going back to L.A. right after the wedding?"

"Maybe a day after the wedding," he told her, raising his voice above the noise of his hammering.

"But you *are* going back?" she pressed, waiting to see just what he'd say.

He paused for a moment, as if weighing something, then said, "Yes, that's the general plan."

She noticed that he kept his back to her when he answered, rather than looking her way. He didn't want to risk making eye contract.

Because he was lying and he knew she'd know it.

It stung her that he was deliberately lying to her. Just for a split second, she thought about telling him that his firm was under the impression that he had taken a leave of absence and that they had told her that at present they had no reentry date for him. But it would only bring about a confrontation and what good would that do?

This wasn't about showing him how smart she was or that she knew he was lying to her. This was supposed to be about giving him enough space to work things out on his own.

Okay, so she'd give him that space.

It felt as if someone was twisting a knife in her gut, but reluctantly, she backed off and let him have his precious space. She could be as patient as the next person, but not infinitely so. If he didn't come clean after his grandfather and Miss Joan left for their honeymoon, she was determined that she and Cash would have words.

Lots and lots of words.

But until then, she'd rein herself in and let things slide. After all, the wedding was only three days away. She could afford to give him three days.

"By the way," she said, changing the subject entirely, "that was a very generous thing you did, paying off the note on your grandfather's ranch."

He shrugged, as if her flattery made him uncomfortable.

"It was the least I could do," he told her. "Seeing as how he initially got into debt because he wanted me to get an education."

"You would have gotten it one way or another," she told him. "It would have just taken you a little longer, that's all."

"Not the point," he said. "He did that for me, without saying a word. I wanted to do the same for him. I would have, too, if Mr. Miller at the bank hadn't caved the way he did."

Alma frowned. "Come again? What does the bank manager have to do with it?"

"I told him I wanted to remain anonymous. I know how proud that old man is and I didn't want him feeling indebted to me. Miller promised it was our little secret. But when my grandfather badgered him, he crumpled like a house of cards in the wind."

She grinned, picturing the scene. "Your grandfather can be pretty persuasive."

Cash got his height from his grandfather. They were both six foot three. "The word is *intimidating*," he corrected.

Grinning, she inclined her head. "There's that, too," Alma conceded.

About to climb farther up on the ladder in order to

continue working on the very top of the arch, Cash shifted on the step and looked down at her. "Did you come here to lend a hand or just to talk and play supervisor?" he asked.

Turning her face up toward his, she pretended to be surprised. "You mean there's a choice?"

"There's always a choice," he answered a bit more seriously than she'd expected.

She'd intended to stay and work all along. "Then I guess I can lend a hand. The sheriff doesn't need the three of us in the office, bumping into one another, anyway. I figure that he can probably spare me for a couple of hours."

"Yeah, he can always put the crime wave on hold for two hours," Cash agreed, then laughed at the very idea of anything remotely close to a crime wave hitting Forever. "I didn't realize how really peaceful it was here until I moved to Los Angeles."

"So I take it that it's *not* the City of Angels?" she teased.

"Oh, there're angels," he told her. "But I think most of the time, they're ducking and hiding to keep from being mowed down." As he positioned the next strip he intended to hammer in, he lifted one shoulder in a half shrug. "Like any city, parts of Los Angeles are beautiful and parts you don't want to walk through, even during the daytime."

"I guess that's why I like it so much here," she confessed. "You could walk anywhere in Forever, night or day, and know that you'll be safe."

"Yeah," he said after a beat. There was a wistful note in his voice.

He was somewhere far away again, Alma thought. Had her words triggered a memory, a thought that took him somewhere against his will?

The expression on Cash's face told her it did.

It took everything she had not to ask him again, not to *demand* to know what was really bothering him.

But soon, she promised herself as she began to work, soon she was going to corner him and make Cash tell her what had invaded his soul to this extent to make him so unhappy.

Chapter Thirteen

When she looked back at it later, Alma decided that the hardest part of pulling off the wedding successfully was keeping to a minimum Miss Joan's participation prior to the actual exchanging of the vows.

That was no easy feat.

Miss Joan kept insisting that she needed to be involved in every aspect of the preparations, from inception to final execution. And, being Miss Joan, everyone had a difficult time trying to persuade her otherwise.

Difficult, but not impossible.

And no one fought harder than Alma to keep the bride in check.

"This isn't the town's annual Christmas party," Alma insisted the morning of the wedding.

She had arrived at Miss Joan's house only to find the woman in her kitchen about to begin preparing the main course at the reception. As gently but firmly as possible, Alma physically removed the older woman from her kitchen and brought her into the bedroom where Tina was waiting for her, curling iron in hand.

"You're not expected to be in charge of everything

and be everywhere at once. This is your *wedding,* Miss Joan," Alma pointed out firmly. "You're supposed to just sit back and let all of us take care of the details for you."

Everyone had gladly pitched in, supplying chairs, decorating the area where their vows were going to be said with flowers, and Olivia—who had discovered a fortuitous aptitude for creative cooking—along with several of the waitresses, had prepared the food to be served at the reception, from appetizers to the main course to the elegant wedding cake.

"But I don't want to just stand on the sidelines. If I have too much time to think, I'm liable to just take off," Miss Joan warned. "I really need to be doing something."

"And you are, Miss Joan," Alma assured her. "You're getting ready for your wedding." She squeezed the woman's icy hands and whispered, "You're just having prewedding jitters, but it's going to be all right," she promised. Ushering the woman into her own bedroom, Alma turned toward Tina. "She's all yours, Tina."

But Miss Joan remained standing rather than sitting down in the chair that Alma had pushed her way. She eyed the curling iron in Tina's hand.

"Just what do you intend to do with that?" she asked.

Because Tina dearly loved the older woman and had seen the softer side of Miss Joan on more than one occasion, she chose her words carefully. "I intend, Miss Joan, to make you even more beautiful than you already are."

Miss Joan sighed, but Alma could see that she was being won over. "I'm not getting all dolled up," she warned. "Harry knows what he's getting. God knows he's unwrapped the package often enough."

But, despite her protest, Miss Joan slowly sank down into the chair and reluctantly turned herself over to Tina.

Tina took her cue and began to deftly apply a little makeup to the wise, weatherworn face before she tackled Miss Joan's rather coarse strawberry-blond hair. "Everyone likes to get dolled up once in a while, Miss Joan," she told her as she worked. "It's human nature."

"Well, I don't," Miss Joan countered stubbornly, squaring her thin shoulders.

Afraid that Miss Joan might just decide to walk out, half-done, Tina put her request on a very personal level. "Then do it for me."

"And for Harry," Alma interjected. "After all, this is a very special day for both of you."

Miss Joan made a funny little skeptical noise that sounded something like a humph.

"And what's that old man doing for me?" she asked, making it sound more like a trade-off than a wedding celebration. She didn't really expect an answer and was rather surprised when Alma actually gave her one.

Alma looked at her watch. "Well, right about now I believe that Cash is trying to help Harry put on his tuxedo—"

"Wait." Miss Joan grabbed Alma's forearm, pulling her in closer. For a woman somewhere in her seventies, she had a grip like the jaws of a pit bull. "Harry's going to be wearing a tuxedo?" she asked incredulously. "Are you sure?"

Alma nodded. "Absolutely. Cash had it sent in from Dallas. It came by special delivery yesterday," she told the woman.

"And he's actually going to wear it?" Miss Joan marveled. Amused, her words were accompanied by a deep chuckle.

Released from Miss Joan's viselike grip, Alma patted the woman's hand. "I heard him say to Cash that he wanted nothing but the best where his lady's concerned." She smiled at the woman. "He really is taken with you, Miss Joan."

Miss Joan did her best not to look as pleased as she was, but she wasn't a hundred percent successful at hiding her reaction.

Clearing her throat, she said, "I guess that old man's got a lick of sense in him after all."

Alma didn't bother hiding her own smile. "I guess so," she agreed.

Tina had finished applying Miss Joan's makeup and picked up the curling iron again. She frowned slightly at the fidgeting woman, who had been like a second mother to her these past couple of years.

"Miss Joan," Tina said tactfully, "if you don't want me burning your head with this thing, I'd appreciate it if you sat still for a few minutes."

Mindful that she'd become a moving target, Miss Joan sighed and then settled down. Like someone in a dentist's chair facing a root canal, she gripped both armrests. "Okay, do your worst," she instructed, bracing herself like a captured soldier in enemy territory awaiting torture.

"I intend to do my very best," Tina contradicted with emphasis as she got started.

Mona peeked into the ever-more crowded bedroom. "How's everything going?" the sheriff's sister asked.

Her question was addressed to Olivia, who had, for the most part, remained silent as she readied Miss Joan's dress for her. Glancing in her direction, Alma saw that Olivia was too busy to realize she was being asked a question, so she answered it for her.

"So far, so good," she told Mona. "We just might be able to pull this off without a hitch."

Mona made her way into the room, careful not to disturb anything or jostle against Tina with her curling iron. She looked up at the wedding dress hanging on the back of the closet door.

"It's not white," she protested in surprise.

This was her first preview of the wedding dress. She'd obviously assumed that Miss Joan would be wearing the traditional white wedding gown. Instead, while very pretty, the dress that Olivia was fussing over was street length and beige. A network of lighter beige lace covered a slightly darker-colored layer of satin. Alma anticipated that Miss Joan would look stunning in it.

"Neither am I," Miss Joan piped up, then clarified, "if you're talking about white standing for purity. This isn't my first time at the dance, you know," she informed the other women. And with that, she thought she'd brought an end to the subject.

She should have known better.

"Why, Miss Joan," Olivia cried, tongue in cheek, "You're making us blush."

"Ha," Miss Joan declared. "And that's meant for the lot of you," she told them. She was sitting as still as she could while Tina circled around her, curling various sections of her hair until she was satisfied with the outcome. "There shouldn't be a blusher in the bunch, seeing the men you've all picked out to go through life with."

The reference made Alma stiffen a little. For her, it acutely brought home the fact that her days with Cash were numbered. He'd said nothing to contradict her assumption—an assumption he actually confirmed— that he was leaving once his grandfather was safely strapped into his seat on the plane bound for Maui.

"You're slipping, Miss Joan," Alma said, trying to sound upbeat. "That doesn't apply to me."

Miss Joan gave her a long, penetrating look. "We'll talk after I get back with my man from that honeymoon your man is sending us on."

It was the woman's wedding day, so Alma didn't bother to contradict her again, but in her heart she felt that she'd just witnessed history being made. Miss Joan—the woman who had never been known to be wrong—was wrong in her assessment that she and Cash were a couple and wrong in her assumption that they were going to go through life that way.

She might love Cash with all her heart—there was no point in denying it—but he would never be her man. That was something she could feel deep down in her gut.

"WELL, THEY DID IT," CASH said, equal parts relief and disbelief echoing in his voice.

The five-piece band Eli had gotten together for the reception was playing something slow and melodic after bringing the walls down with their first four numbers. Before he realized what he was doing, Cash had taken Alma by the hand and led her onto the dance floor that he and Alma's brothers had labored to finish in time.

He had his arm around her waist and her hand tucked into his as he pressed it against his chest. They were swaying in time to a song whose title escaped him.

Not that he was really trying to remember.

He was still very much focused on the fact that the wedding had actually come off without a hitch. He felt a great deal of pride in having had a hand in that.

And, he marveled not for the first time, he had never seen his grandfather looking so incredibly happy before. This had to be what he had been like as a young man, Cash surmised. Harry was certainly behaving as if the years had magically melted away from him, leaving in its wake a man in the prime of his life.

At least for today.

"Yes, it all went really well, thanks to you," she reminded him. She saw the protest hovering on his lips and talked quickly to silence it. "If you hadn't talked her down, Miss Joan would have bolted, taking the next bus out of here." Her eyes met his. "I think you know that."

Cash refused to take credit for that. "She would have come to her senses."

"I don't know about that." Her eyes hadn't left his. "Fear makes people do funny things," she said pointedly.

Her words echoed in his head for a moment and he looked at her. Was she talking about him, or was there something more to her words?

"Are you speaking from experience?" Cash asked.

"No, from observation," she countered. Alma paused for a moment, taking in a long breath.

Okay, here we go, opening a door, she told herself. Out loud, she said, "You know you can always tell me anything, right?"

"Yes, I know." Swaying with her like this was beginning to unravel him. He was grateful that they were out in front of everyone so he couldn't act on his emotions. "I also know that I can be quiet around you, that neither one of us has to say a word and it doesn't feel awkward. It feels comfortable," he concluded.

That was his way of telling her to back off, Alma thought.

Since this was Miss Joan and Harry's wedding day, she had no choice but to do exactly that for now. She wouldn't say anything that might escalate into a scene and ruin this day for two people she cared about.

But this wasn't the end of it.

She had no intentions of backing off and giving up. Her plan was the complete opposite. She intended to keep at him until he finally let her into his inner sanctum and she could help him get over whatever it was that he needed to put behind him. She didn't care how long it took or what she had to do, but she was determined to bring Cash back to the land of the living.

Another slow song began a beat after the last one ended. The band was probably tired, but she didn't care. It gave her an excuse to stay in his arms a little longer and there was no place she would rather have been.

Well, maybe one other place, but he was included in that, too, she thought with a secret smile.

As a counterbeat to the music, a distant rumble resounded.

Picking her head up from his shoulder, Alma looked in the direction the thunder had come from. They'd been on the verge of a storm all day and although they still dearly needed rain, Alma had kept her fingers crossed that if it was coming, the rain would hold off until after the reception.

The sky had cooperated only for the actual wedding ceremony, clearing up long enough for the bride to walk down the makeshift aisle to the even more makeshift altar where Harry, resplendent in the tuxedo Cash had bought for him, stood waiting for her and beaming brighter than a lighthouse beacon.

Reference to that effect were actually Miss Joan's first words to her husband-to-be when she reached the flower-laced altar.

"Stop grinning like some damn village idiot, Harry," she'd hissed.

"Can't help it," he'd answered loud enough for half the gathering to hear. "I've never seen you looking this beautiful before."

She made the same dismissive noise she'd made in her bedroom that morning, but it was obvious to anyone who was watching that Harry's compliment pleased her beyond all words.

Alma scanned the sky now. Twilight slowly spread its cloak around the town. "That doesn't sound promising," she said.

"Hasn't rained here so far this summer," Cash pointed out. "Odds are it probably won't now."

"You know it hasn't rained here?" she asked.

He could tell what she was thinking. That she'd just assumed he'd divorced himself from everything that had to do with Forever.

"No law against my following the local weather reports," he told her.

"Just surprised that you would, that's all," she admitted. "Seeing as how you haven't been back even once in all this time."

"Couldn't," he replied, avoiding her eyes. "Too much work to do."

"In ten years, you couldn't find even a few days?" she asked incredulously. That certainly didn't seem possible. *Nobody* worked that hard, not without some serious consequences.

So much for quietly dropping the subject. Cash looked at her. In the background, the song the band was playing was softly fading away.

"Seriously?" he asked her. "You want to fight now? Here?"

"I'm not fighting," Alma contradicted, trying very hard not to let her temper climb. "I'm just asking a question."

The song over, he released her. Alma obviously waited for an answer. Cash blew out an impatient breath.

"All right, then, I'll answer that question. I couldn't find the time because I was laying down the groundwork for my future—or thought I was," he said with frustration.

She didn't quite understand the tension in his voice. What wasn't he saying? "But you weren't?" she asked.

It was far too complicated to get into now even if he wanted to—and he didn't. All he wanted to do was just enjoy this last bit of time alone with her. Tomorrow, he'd be gone. He had to be.

If he stayed, it was simply a matter of time before he made love with Alma again—and again. And his feelings about that hadn't changed. It wouldn't be fair to her. He wasn't free to love her the way she deserved to be loved: completely and honestly.

He had no right to be happy and he had no right to bring her down with him, so the only solution was for him to leave. But he didn't want to talk about any of that, not now. He wanted to pretend, for a few hours longer, that everything would work itself out.

"Put your head against my chest, shut up and dance," he instructed as the band began to play again. It was a country song about having regrets. He couldn't help thinking how appropriate that was.

Deciding to lighten the mood and table the discussion for now, Alma said, "You had me at 'put your head against my chest,' but you nearly lost me at 'shut up.' The dance part is weighing in a little more on the first side," she said.

Cash laughed shortly as he shook his head. "You are definitely one of a kind, Alma Rodriguez." His arm closed around her waist and he brought her closer to him. His body heated accordingly. He didn't care. Tomorrow this would be in the past. And so would she.

He blocked the ache that was taking root in his heart. "Sometimes I forget just how really unique you are."

"There's a remedy for that," she quipped.

He held her to him, moving in time to the tempo. "We'll discuss that later," he promised, knowing that for them, there would be no later. She would thank him for that—in another forty years or so.

As the band continued to play, Cash closed his eyes and let himself go. Just for the smallest moment, he allowed himself to pretend that he had never left Forever. That he hadn't become a criminal lawyer with an incredible track record for winning cases, but had stayed right where he was, becoming a rancher. That he spent each day breaking in quarter horses and battling Mother Nature. It was a damn sight better than having to battle his conscience.

Because there was no winning in that case.

Thunder rumbled, more loudly this time, causing the band to momentarily stop playing. It was obvious that they were debating running for shelter with their instruments, just in case.

One beat after the thunder crashed, the sky suddenly lit up, looking as bright as day as a long, jagged bolt of lightning creased its brow, touching down not more than a couple of miles away from where they were standing.

"That was almost too close for comfort," Alma said as the band hesitantly began to play again.

Alma had just laid her head against his chest again and begun to sway once more to the music when she felt Cash suddenly stiffening.

Puzzled, she raised her head and looked at him quizzically.

"My guess is so's that," he said, confusing her even more.

He was pointing to something over her head and off in the distance. When she turned to look, she saw exactly what he was referring to.

A thick column of black smoke, pushed ever upward by orange-yellow flames, was reaching into the very same sky that the lightning had brightened only moments ago.

And then someone cried something that everyone lived in fear of every day.

"Fire!"

Chapter Fourteen

The mood at the reception transformed from joyous to alarmed and anxious. Everyone knew the threat of an uncontained fire. There wasn't a person among them who hadn't either gone through the devastation that a fire generated or knew someone who had.

The moment the cry of "fire" was heard, approximately one-third of the people there ceased being wedding guests and became active members of Forever's all-volunteer fire department.

Like so many other small towns around the country, Forever couldn't support an official fire department. Instead, the town relied on volunteers, residents of Forever who gave up one to two days a month to train how to fight fires as conscientiously as any professional firefighter. They did it so that if the need actually arose, they would be prepared.

Rick Santiago did double duty, serving as both the sheriff of the town and the fire chief.

The new bride and groom were as horrified and concerned as everyone else about the possible consequences of the blaze they saw.

"We need to do something," Miss Joan cried, clasping Harry's hand.

Overhearing, Cash said, "What you need to do is go to the airport and get on that plane so you can start your honeymoon."

"We can't leave at a time like this," Harry protested.

"Don't worry, it'll be handled," Alma assured the couple. She saw the stubborn look that entered Miss Joan's eyes. "Dad, could you do everyone a really big favor and drive these two kids to the airport before their good intentions get them in trouble?"

Miguel nodded. "I can do that. C'mon, you two," he said, placing himself between the couple and taking each by the elbow. "When she starts to talk like that, there's no winning with her," he said with feeling. "So don't even try."

Relieved that all three would be out of harm's way, Alma turned back to what was going on.

Rick had stepped up and was calling for the others who volunteered regularly with him.

"C'mon, c'mon," he shouted above the din of anxious, concerned voices. "We've got to get down to the fire station and get rolling before that fire starts to spread."

As Alma started to run toward the front of the house and the cars that were parked there, Cash suddenly grabbed her arm.

He had a bad feeling about this. "Where are you going?" he asked.

She would have thought that was self-evident. "With

Rick and the others. To fight the fire," she added when he continued to stare at her.

"But it's not safe," Cash protested.

There was no arguing that, she thought, but this wasn't exactly the time to start weighing the pros and cons.

"I'm part of the volunteer fire department," she told Cash. "All the deputies are." She could see that came as a complete surprise to him. Didn't he remember what things were like when he lived here? Forever had never had a town-funded fire department. "You're not in Los Angeles, Cash. We don't have a regular fire department, remember?" She pulled her arm free of his grip. "Now, if you don't mind, I've got to go."

He might have let go of her arm, but now Cash was running right alongside her. It was her turn to ask, "Where are *you* going?"

"I'm going with you," he answered simply as they reached the front.

She stopped and turned toward him, her body blocking his ability to go any farther. "Cash, I appreciate your concern, really," she said tactfully, "but I've had training. You haven't."

"I'll wing it," he said, unfazed.

The way he saw it, if Alma was determined to get into harm's way, he was just as determined to be there and watch over her as best he could. Being a deputy in a sleepy-eyed town was one thing, but little town or not, fighting a fire was really dangerous.

At the front of the house Rick, Joe and the town

doctor, their most recent volunteer to join up, were dividing up the group, each taking as many people in their cars as they could.

When he saw Cash coming with Alma, Rick abruptly stopped shouting orders. Coming over to them, it was obvious by his expression that he was questioning Cash's intentions.

Cash answered his question before it was asked. "I'm coming with you," he told the sheriff. "There's got to be something I can do to help."

"Always glad to have another able-bodied citizen along," Rick said, emphasizing the word *citizen*.

Cash didn't seem to notice as he climbed into Rick's car, but Alma did.

The fire station, where the volunteers periodically trained, was located on the outskirts of town. Along with training manuals and a makeshift dummy building where they set small fires to practice on, the station also housed a freshly repainted fire truck that had once been used to fight fires in Austin.

Through his connections Rick had managed to buy the old truck for a song. It had been deemed outmoded and was being shipped out to meet its demise in a junkyard. The truck was in truly bad condition but Rick had become an optimist along the way and he'd had the truck shipped back to Forever. When it arrived, he'd turned the barely running vehicle over to Forever's only resident mechanic, Mick Henley. Mick performed a miracle or two, raised the truck from the dead and turned it into their first line of defense when it came to fighting the fires that perennially plagued the region.

Rick drove the truck to the site of the fire. As many of the volunteers as could fit piled into the truck. The rest followed in their own vehicles, or hitched a ride with a friend.

They didn't have far to go.

Lightning had struck Silas Varner's Hardware Store and the two houses that were on either side of it. The houses belonged to Varner, as well. He lived in one and his widower son, Steve, lived in the other with his little boys. Like his father, Steve put in long hours at the hardware store.

The store was already half-consumed by the flames, and the houses, both two-story and several decades old, appeared destined for the same fate.

After bringing the truck to a grinding halt, Rick was the first one on the ground. He began ordering everyone to their posts.

Because the county water district had refitted all the pipelines beneath the town eighteen months ago, getting water to the source of the fire was not a problem. But whether or not the fire could be put out in time to save anything still remained to be seen.

Silas Varner stumbled out of his house just as the fire truck pulled up in front of his store. He was coughing so hard that for several minutes he couldn't say a coherent word.

When he could finally speak, looking desperate and

wild-eyed, he grabbed the first person's arm that he came to. It was Cash.

"My boy's still inside his house and my grandsons—" His voice broke and he couldn't finish his sentence, but he didn't have to.

"We'll get them," Rick assured him. Looking around, he raised his voice to get Dan's attention. "Doc, we could use you over here."

"No, that's okay. I'm all right, I'm all right," Silas protested weakly. "Just get my son and grandsons," he pleaded.

"We will," Joe promised the man, hurrying to join Rick.

Within a moment, Dan had pushed his way through the cluster of bodies in order to reach Silas.

The older man's face was a mask of fear. He watched as Rick sent three of the volunteers into the younger Varner's house to find Steve and his two small sons. Other volunteers were dispatched to work the unwieldy fire hose and aim it at the burning buildings. Since the hardware store presented the greatest threat, the men focused their efforts on it.

Those who weren't working the hose shoved dirt onto the perimeter of the fire, trying to suffocate the smaller flames before they had a chance to grow into bigger ones.

Because Cash had no training, Rick had put him on the latter detail. Cash did what he was able, shoveling as fast as he could.

When he stepped back for a moment, trying to get

out of the way of some flying burning debris, he looked up and saw that one of Varner's grandsons was in the second-story window. The blond-haired boy, no more than about four, looked absolutely terrified.

Cash looked around for Rick or someone he could point out the boy to, but everyone was either converged around the truck, doing what they could to put out the fire, or they were on opposite sides of the buildings, shoveling dirt.

At that moment, he saw the three volunteers rushing out of the front door, a sheet of flames right behind them as two of the men carried Steve Varner out between them. The third volunteer, Joe, was carrying the older grandson in his arms.

Taking in the scene and processing his options quickly, Cash felt that the trapped boy's only chance to get out would be through the window, not through the house. From the looks of it, going back in that way wasn't possible anymore.

Driving up, he'd taken note of a tall oak tree that was towering over Steve's house. It was standing not far from the side where the boy was trapped. With just a little bit of luck, Cash judged, he could use the tree to get to the boy.

It took Cash exactly five seconds to come up with his plan and then implement it. Running to the tree, he began to climb up.

That was when Alma saw him.

As she screamed out his name, hoping to stop him, she saw the terrified little boy.

Now she understood.

Her heart froze halfway up her throat. Cash might be able to get to the boy, but then how was he going to get back into the tree with him?

Frantic, Alma could only stare and pray as she watched Cash make his way up. He slipped twice and she was certain he was going to fall, but he didn't. Somehow, in what felt like an eternity later, he made it to the edge of the branch. It bowed dangerously beneath his weight. Cash inched his way along until he came to the end of it. About a foot shy of the window.

Because it was summer and hot, the window was open. Otherwise, Cash sincerely doubted that the boy would have been able to get it open on his own.

"C'mon, boy, just lean out the window," he urged, stretching out his arms. "You can do it. I'll catch you."

"No," the little boy screamed, crying. "I'll fall. I'll fall," he said over and over again.

Cash sighed. He hadn't come up just to stay on the limb and watch the boy die. Taking a deep breath, he propelled himself forward in a pseudoleap and barely managed to get hold of the windowsill with his fingertips.

The splintered wood pierced his skin as he struggled to hang on. His forearms and biceps screamed in protest as he managed to pull himself up and inside the burning building.

Once he did, Cash grabbed the boy in his arms and then looked back out. Leaping back wasn't possible, not if he had to hold on to the boy, but there didn't seem to be another option open to them.

"Cash! Cash, down here!"

There was ringing in his ears and the fire roared behind him. His very clothing got hot and the metal of his belt buckle felt as if it was branding his skin.

He had to be hallucinating. He could have sworn he heard Alma calling his name.

"Cash! Look down here!"

This time, it was the sheriff's voice that resonated above the noise. He looked down and saw that Alma, Rick and five other volunteers had stretched out what appeared to be a tarp between them. They were holding it taut.

"Jump!" Alma cried. "We'll catch you!"

From where he was, it didn't look likely, but it was probably the only chance he and the boy had to survive.

Leaning forward, Cash held the boy out. "The boy first!" he told them. But when he went to release the child, he found that the terrified little boy had a death grip around his neck. "C'mon, boy, you have to let go of me."

But the boy just held on tighter, so much so that he was beginning to cut off Cash's air. "No! I don't wanna die," he sobbed.

"You're not going to die. I won't let you," Cash assured him, doing his best to sound cheerful, hoping the boy would respond to his tone. "This is just like a parachute drop at an amusement park," he told him. "There's nothing to it and they're all waiting to catch you," he promised. "Nobody's going to let anything happen to you. You can be sure of that. Remember, I'm the guy who just leaped in to save you," he added with a wink.

He felt the little boy's grip begin to loosen just a little.

Steve Varner pushed forward until he was just beneath the second-story window. "C'mon, Jackie, jump," he coaxed. "You can do it, boy. Just pretend it's Daddy's bed and you're jumping up and down, the way you and Jimmy always do. C'mon," he pleaded. "Jump!"

The boy timidly released his hold on Cash's neck. Cash immediately dropped him, aiming as close to the center of the tarp as he possibly could.

The second the child hit the tarp, the volunteers lowered it so that Jackie could stand up and run to his father. He was off in a flash.

"Did ya see me, Daddy? Did ya see? I jumped," he declared proudly, stretching out the word.

Steve could only hold the boy close and do his best not to sob.

An ominous noise resounded from the burning building Cash was still stranded in, as walls, consumed by the fire, began to crumble into hot ashes.

The building was coming down.

And Cash with it.

"Get it up!" Alma screamed. "Get the tarp up! Now!" The volunteers she'd corralled immediately lifted the tarp up a second time, bringing it as close to the second house as they dared.

They got it up as the entire second building collapsed.

Cash just managed to clear the window before it and everything else in the building shuddered and then came crashing down. He landed on the tarp, singed, coughing up smoke and feeling more than a little lightheaded.

Alma rushed to him and threw her arms around Cash. A half second later, Cash's knees buckled and he blacked out.

The weight of his body almost caused her to fall over, as well. She struggled to remain upright, her shoulder propped up beneath Cash's arm.

He was unconscious.

Worried, Alma cried, "A little help here." Within a minute Rick, Dan and Joe were removing Cash's deadweight from her.

Rick and Joe laid the unconscious Cash down on the ground, away from the burning houses and store, as Dan did a quick medical assessment.

"He'll be all right," Dan assured Alma, gaining his feet again. "A little ointment on those burns, a little bed rest and your hero'll be good as new."

Her hero.

He was that, she thought. He always had been.

Tears zigzagged their way down her soot-covered cheeks. The dress she had on was covered with soot, burned in places and utterly beyond repair. It was ruined, as were her matching shoes.

But, all things considered, Alma couldn't remember

when she'd felt happier. Cash was all right. He was going to live and he was all right.

With a lump in her throat, she found that she could barely push out her words of thanks to the doctor.

Dan smiled at her. "I'm not the one who did anything," he said as he closed his medical bag. Nodding his head at Cash, he said, "He did."

Rick, who along with Joe and Larry had gone back to join the rest of the firefighters still battling the fire, suddenly came running back to them.

"We've got to get him up," he shouted to Dan and Alma before he reached them.

She knew that Cash belonged in a bed right now, but the urgency in Rick's voice told her that his order had nothing to do Cash's actual condition. From the sound of it, something else was very wrong.

Now what?

"Why?" she wanted to know.

"Silas just told me that he got in a large shipment of varnish and paint remover yesterday. If the fire gets to them, there's going to be one hell of a huge explosion. I want everyone who isn't fighting the fire to clear out! Now!" he shouted. "That's an order."

The next second he was pivoting on his heel and running back to the fire truck and his men.

Alma was torn between running after Rick to try to get the fire under control and out before the unthinkable happened, and going in the opposite direction, dragging Cash to safety with Dan's help.

In the end, she went with her heart and Cash.

Between the two of them, she and Dan got Cash onto his feet and over to where the vehicles were parked. One of the cars belonged to Eli.

"Go," she told Dan once they'd gotten Cash into the backseat. "I can handle it from here. The sheriff's going to need everyone he can get."

The fire that had consumed Steve Varner's house had been contained and was almost out and they seemed to have gotten a handle on the other house fire, but the fire at the hardware store was as ominous as ever.

Dan appeared a little skeptical as he glanced at his patient again. "Are you sure you can manage him on your own?"

She nodded, then smiled. "In case you haven't noticed yet, Doctor, they grow their women tough out here." She had a feeling she knew what he was thinking and added, "Even the short ones."

"I'll take you at your word," he said. "Like I said, he should be fine by morning. But if he's not, or you have any doubts, give me a call. Night or day," he added.

"Like the doctors of old," she quipped. "The ones that people said used to make house calls."

"Exactly like the doctors of old," he told her. The next moment, he turned on his heel and ran back to the fire truck—and the fire.

Chapter Fifteen

He was there again.

Back in the courtroom, defending Ronald Harper. Winning the freedom of the man accused of killing a husband and wife during a robbery.

Securing Harper's freedom not on hard and fast evidence, or even lack of hard and fast evidence, but on a technicality. The police had found the murder weapon in Harper's bottom bureau drawer—a closed bureau drawer—without the benefit of a search warrant. Because of that, he'd gotten the judge to rule that the weapon was inadmissible as evidence. And, just like that, the case was thrown out of court.

Standing there, Cash watched Harper as the man strolled by him, a smirk on his lips.

And that was when he knew.

Knew that despite the man's swearing on a stack of Bibles that he was innocent, Ronald Harper had killed those two young people.

Within the blink of an eye, Cash found himself transported to a street corner in a residential area, watching several policemen firing at Harper. He saw Harper, wearing that same smirk, sink to his knees, five police-issued bullets piercing his body. He was dead before he hit the ground.

But not before he'd ended the lives of a family of five whose home he had invaded. A family who would still be alive if he hadn't gotten Harper off.

Five faces swirled around him, all crying the same thing. "You killed us." Shaking, in a puddle of sweat, Cash bolted upright, yelling, "No!"

"Easy there, hero," Alma said soothingly. Her hands on his chest, she pushed Cash gently back down onto the bed and tucked the sheet around him.

Cash's eyes looked almost wild as he took in his surroundings. As they registered, he calmed down a little. He wasn't in court, or out on that street corner. He was inside Alma's bedroom.

In her bed?

How?

Cash had no recollection of coming here. The last thing he remembered was trying to get that boy out of the burning building. Fragments came back to him like bits and pieces in a kaleidoscope.

He gazed back at Alma again. "What am I doing here?" he asked.

"Hopefully recovering," Alma answered, trying to keep her voice light. Then, because he was still looking at her intently, she explained, "My place was closer than your grandfather's ranch, so I had the sheriff and my brothers bring you here two days ago."

The information stunned him. "Two da— I've been

out for two days?" That couldn't be possible. She had to be mistaken.

"Two days," she confirmed. "The doctor stopped by a couple of times to look in on you. He told me that these things take time, that you'd come around." But she wasn't nearly as patient as she looked. "I have to admit, though, I was getting kind of worried."

There was a burning sensation through his lungs and throat. Taking in a deep breath made it ache even more. He drew the next one in more slowly.

"And you've been here the whole time?" he asked, surprised.

Alma half shrugged, half nodded. "I put the town's crime wave on hold again." She offered him a smile, doing her best to hide how worried she'd been, how very relieved she was now to see him open his eyes. "Didn't seem like anything else was as important as being here when you woke up.

"Mr. Varner and his son came by to see how you were doing yesterday," she said by way of a footnote. "They asked to be notified the minute you came to, but I think you'd rather have a little time to pull yourself together first."

"Yeah," Cash agreed absently. His chest was really aching, as if a tree trunk or something equally heavy had fallen across it. He felt as exhausted as he had the time he'd finished his first ten-K run. "What did you call me when I woke up?" he asked suddenly, confused as words popped up at random in his brain.

"I said, 'Easy there, hero,'" Alma repeated.

The scowl that appeared on his face went down clear to the bone. "I'm not a hero," Cash snapped.

The flash of anger surprised her. Maybe they should have taken Cash to the hospital. It was a fifty-mile drive, but maybe he needed an X-ray or lab tests.

"I'm afraid Mr. Varner and his family would beg to differ with that assessment. When he was here yesterday, Silas kept talking about giving you free tools for life."

None of this was making any sense to him. "Why? Why would he say something like that?"

Had he hit his head when he'd jumped? Or had the smoke somehow addled his brain?

"In case you've forgotten," she said gently, "you did an imitation of a flying squirrel and saved his younger grandson, Jack. There's no way to actually repay someone for saving a life, but Silas is determined to give it a try."

Cash looked away, the nightmare he'd had still lingering around the perimeter of his brain. It was impossible to shake and it reinforced the weight of the guilt.

"There's no way to make up for losing one, either," he told her.

He was obviously referring to whatever it was that haunted him. She was through waiting for him to volunteer the information on his own.

"Okay," she informed him, pulling the chair she'd occupied for the past two days closer to the bed. "I've been patient long enough. You tell me what's eating away at you or you don't get out of this room." She saw the skeptical expression that entered Cash's eyes. "I'm not bluffing. If you care to glance under the sheet, you'll notice that you're not exactly dressed for a stroll in our fair streets," she told him. "I've got your pants and I intend to hold them for ransom until you tell me what I want to know."

Cash shook his head, trying to protect her and, he supposed, himself, as well. She would look at him with hatred once she knew and he couldn't bear that. "You don't want to know this."

They were beyond teasing, beyond banter. When she looked at him, there was no smile on her lips. Her eyes met his.

"Oh, yes, I do. You're in pain, Cash, and you have been ever since you got here. I want to know why."

The pause was so long she was certain he wasn't going to answer her. Just as she moved in for another attack, he began to talk. His voice had a hard, unforgiving edge to it. "I helped a killer beat a murder charge."

It was her understanding that this was what he did for a living. He was a defense lawyer whose firm dealt with high-profile criminal cases.

"Did you know he was a killer at the time you defended him?" she asked.

He sighed, thinking. Pulling the pieces together. "Not for certain," he allowed. "But looking back, I had my suspicions," Cash admitted.

"What happened?" Alma prodded, knowing there had to be more to the story.

"Three weeks after the trial was over, he was caught

breaking into another house. A neighbor called the police, said she heard screaming. They showed up in spades. He tried to shoot his way out and the police wound up having to kill him." He took in a deep breath. His chest ached even more.

"There's more to it than that." Her intuition told her as much. He wouldn't have been this distraught over the death of a career criminal. "What aren't you telling me?"

"The police killed him, but not before he killed a family of five. Mother and father, two teenage boys and a four-year-old girl." He closed his eyes for a moment, the torment of that knowledge almost too much for him to handle. "If I hadn't gotten that scum off, the family would still be alive. I killed them, Alma," he cried. "Ronald Harper might have been the one who pulled the actual trigger, but I'm the one who killed them, who's responsible for their deaths."

His guilt was palatable and her heart ached for him. "Things don't always play out the way we want them to."

He knew she meant well, but he couldn't get his bitterness—directed at himself—under control. "Yeah, well, you tell that to that family. Oops, sorry, I didn't mean for this to happen, but you're dead. My bad."

She watched him pointedly, deliberately abandoning any sympathy she'd been feeling for him. He didn't need coddling, he needed a way to get back to the surface before he buried himself alive.

"So now what? You're going to beat yourself up for the rest of your life?"

He blew out a breath, then shrugged. "Sounds like a plan."

She pulled no punches. "Sounds like a lousy plan," Alma told him.

"You don't get a say in it," he told her, trying very hard to make her back away from him. She would only be letting herself in for disappointment if she stayed in his life.

That stung but this wasn't about her; it was about him and he was hurting badly. She had to get him to see past the pain, see the uselessness of what he was doing to himself.

"Maybe not, but let me ask you a question. Say you go on beating yourself up." She gave him the full treatment. "You even put on a hair shirt, sleep on coals, walk on glass—is *any* of this going to bring back even *one* member of that family?" When he didn't say anything, she demanded, "Well, is it?"

There was anger in his eyes when he looked at her. "No."

"Okay, we've established that," she said, her voice devoid of emotion as she continued. "Now let's establish something else. Two nights ago you saved a little boy's life, a little boy who, if not for your insane superhero act, would now be laid out in a casket, waiting to be the central figure in a funeral. You *saved* a life," she stressed. "Maybe that's how you're supposed to learn to live with yourself, learn to forgive yourself."

He wasn't following the point she was trying to make. "I leap into burning buildings?"

Alma was willing to grasp at any straw. "Should the occasion arise, maybe, yeah. But until then, you put your mind to doing something positive with what you have to work with."

That might have sounded good on paper, but he had nothing to offer. "Like what?"

She thought of Olivia. "Like donate some of your time to helping people who are in a bind but can't afford a lawyer. Lots of ways to save a life, Cash. Not all of them involve leaping into burning buildings. Some of them involve helping someone to *get* a life. Or get a second chance in life." She'd warmed to her subject and was talking faster and more earnestly. "You could do a lot of good, Cash, if you just get over yourself."

"Get over myself?" he repeated incredulously, staring at Alma. "You make it sound as if I enjoy feeling this way."

"Well, maybe not 'enjoy,'" she allowed. "But sitting in the dark, hating yourself, is a lot easier than going into the light and *doing* something positive."

She was desperately trying to keep him from sinking into a bottomless depression. She'd seen the same expression that was now in Cash's eyes in Edwin Walker's eyes when he lost his wife of forty-three years. The rancher sank into a depression and never surfaced again. The sheriff found him floating in the river a year after his wife died. She wasn't about to let something like that happen to Cash.

She took Cash's hand in hers, as if willing him some of her energy.

"You've got a lot to offer, Cash. Don't just throw it all away." She looked into his eyes and whispered, "Please."

Maybe he could make it, he thought. But to do it, he needed her at his side, he knew that. And he had no right to expect it.

"Why are you being so understanding?" he asked. "I abandoned you."

Alma shrugged. The past was the past and it was time to let go. "You were young. Stupid, yes, but young."

He shook his head. "It's no excuse."

Alma smiled at him. All she ever wanted from Cash was an apology—that and to have him come back to Forever. And, from where she was standing, it seemed to her as if she had just gotten both, just not in so many words.

"Work with me here," she told him. "I'm on your side, even if you're not," she added.

He knew that now, and should have known it back then. "I think my first mistake was to forget just how good you could make me feel about everything."

"Well, you can reflect on that while you're recuperating. Doc wants you to get a couple of days' bed rest," she emphasized. "I can have him come by later today to give you a once-over now that you're conscious, but he did say that he thought the best thing for you was just to rest."

"Just to rest," he echoed.

"Yes."

"Here, in this bed." It wasn't exactly a question, but it wasn't a statement, either.

This was the bed they'd made love in. Still, she played out the line. "Well, it seems to only make sense, since you're already lying in it."

"This is your bed."

Alma shrugged. God knew she wasn't territorial, and right now he was the one who needed to get his strength back.

"I'll sleep in the chair. Or on the floor. I've got a sleeping bag in the closet," she told him. "And I can more or less sleep anywhere."

"How about in your own bed?" he suggested, patting the place next to him. "There's plenty of room for two people." He raised his eyes to hers, a seductive glimmer in them. "Remember?"

Alma grinned. She had a feeling things would be all right after all. "Something tells me from the gleam in your eyes that getting your rest suddenly isn't exactly uppermost in your mind."

"Suddenly, no, it's not." For the first time since he'd woken up, he felt alive. His eyes skimmed over the length of her. "But what I am thinking of will definitely help speed up my recovery."

"The doctor didn't mention anything about undertaking gymnastics," she said, doing her best to keep a straight face.

"You can be on top," he told her. "What you do with that position is strictly up to you."

Alma laughed and shook her head again. "You sound like you're feeling better." And she couldn't have been more relieved or happier about it.

"*You* make me feel better," he told her with feeling. "Being with you makes me remember a better time."

She kissed him lightly on the lips. "That time can be now, Cash. It doesn't have to exist only in the past." Alma cupped his cheek. "You want to atone for that sin you feel you committed? Do an occasional good deed. Help a person who otherwise would have nowhere to turn."

She made it all sound so easy. "You're right," he told her. But he was a realist. "I can't do it without you."

"Who says you have to?" she asked. "You know where to find me."

He'd known all along and been an idiot about it, Cash thought. It was time he owned up to that and made up for the time he'd lost. "I'd like to not have to look."

"What?" She wasn't sure what he was trying to tell her, and she was even more afraid of jumping to the wrong conclusion.

"As in my coming home to you," he told her. "Every night."

"Are you…?" He was, she realized. He was asking her to marry him. This wasn't a town where people just lived with one another. "How addled is your brain, anyway?"

Cash threaded his fingers through her hair. Why

had he been fighting this for so long? They belonged together. She was the other half of his soul, she always had been. "Not enough for me not to know what I'm saying," he assured her.

Okay, if he'd come this far, then she wanted to hear the actual words. "Which is…?"

His eyes held hers, and his world, he realized, came completely together. "Marry me, Alma."

She got up and reached for the telephone on the nightstand. "I think I'd better get ahold of the doctor and have him come over now."

He caught her hand and stopped her from picking up the receiver.

"He has his own wife. I'm serious, Alma. Marry me. I wanted to ask you to marry me the second I walked into town and saw you. The only thing stopping me was that I didn't feel I had the right to be with someone like you. Not after what I'd done."

As thrilled as she was to have him actually ask her to marry him, she knew this really wasn't right. It was too much like taking advantage of him. She wanted him to ask her when he wasn't suffering from smoke inhalation.

"You're on an emotional roller coaster and not thinking too clearly right now," she told him. Damn but this noble stuff wasn't easy, especially when all she wanted to do was throw her arms around him and kiss him until they both couldn't breathe. When she'd seen him leap into the burning house through the window, she'd been terrified that she'd lost him for good. "Two days from now you'll wake up and regret asking me."

"What I'll regret two days from now is that I didn't ask you to marry me sooner." And then a thought hit him right in the pit of his stomach. What if she was saying this because their time together had passed? What if she didn't want to marry him? "Unless, of course, you turn me down." He watched her eyes as he talked. "That, I could have lived for years without confirming."

Had he lost his mind? Or did he really not know her anymore? "You honestly think I'd turn you down?"

He wanted to say no, but he wasn't a hundred percent sure. "You've got every right to get revenge after the way I treated you."

He was serious. Wow. Alma sighed, then thrust her hand out to him. "Hello, I don't think we've been introduced. My name is Alma. What's yours?"

He laughed, knowing that she was telling him that if he believed any of what he'd just said, then he really didn't know her.

But he did.

And he was looking forward to remaining forever in Forever, getting to know her even better. And loving the process.

For the first time in a long time, he felt that things were going to be all right after all. He'd told her his deep, dark secret and instead of being repulsed, or even horrified by what he'd said, she was determined to stick by his side and help him.

He didn't deserve her, but Cash silently promised her that he would spend the rest of his life making her not regret her decision.

"I love you, Alma," he said with feeling.

Alma's eyes crinkled as she grinned broadly at him. The happiness she felt radiating inside her seemed almost too great to contain. "I guess you finally *have* come to your senses. I love you, too, you big idiot. And after you get back to normal, I'm going to enjoy showing you just how much."

"I need a preview," he said solemnly. "Something to hold on to."

"A preview," she repeated, and he nodded. "Okay, I guess that could be arranged." Slipping under the covers, Alma turned her body toward his. Her eyes were shining as she said, "One hot preview coming up."

* * * * *

HEART & HOME

Harlequin®

American ★ Romance®

COMING NEXT MONTH
AVAILABLE JUNE 12, 2012

#1405 BET ON A COWBOY
Julie Benson

#1406 RODEO DAUGHTER
Fatherhood
Leigh Duncan

#1407 THE RANCHER'S BRIDE
Pamela Britton

#1408 MONTANA DOCTOR
Saddlers Prairie
Ann Roth

HARCNM0512

REQUEST YOUR FREE BOOKS!
2 FREE NOVELS PLUS 2 FREE GIFTS!

Harlequin

American ★ Romance

LOVE, HOME & HAPPINESS

YES! Please send me 2 FREE Harlequin® American Romance® novels and my 2 FREE gifts (gifts are worth about $10). After receiving them, if I don't wish to receive any more books, I can return the shipping statement marked "cancel." If I don't cancel, I will receive 4 brand-new novels every month and be billed just $4.49 per book in the U.S. or $5.24 per book in Canada. That's a saving of at least 14% off the cover price! It's quite a bargain! Shipping and handling is just 50¢ per book in the U.S. and 75¢ per book in Canada.* I understand that accepting the 2 free books and gifts places me under no obligation to buy anything. I can always return a shipment and cancel at any time. Even if I never buy another book, the two free books and gifts are mine to keep forever.

154/354 HDN FEP2

Name _____ (PLEASE PRINT)

Address _____ Apt. #

City _____ State/Prov. _____ Zip/Postal Code

Signature (if under 18, a parent or guardian must sign)

Mail to the **Reader Service:**
IN U.S.A.: P.O. Box 1867, Buffalo, NY 14240-1867
IN CANADA: P.O. Box 609, Fort Erie, Ontario L2A 5X3

Not valid for current subscribers to Harlequin American Romance books.

Want to try two free books from another line?
Call 1-800-873-8635 or visit www.ReaderService.com.

* Terms and prices subject to change without notice. Prices do not include applicable taxes. Sales tax applicable in N.Y. Canadian residents will be charged applicable taxes. Offer not valid in Quebec. This offer is limited to one order per household. All orders subject to credit approval. Credit or debit balances in a customer's account(s) may be offset by any other outstanding balance owed by or to the customer. Please allow 4 to 6 weeks for delivery. Offer available while quantities last.

Your Privacy—The Reader Service is committed to protecting your privacy. Our Privacy Policy is available online at www.ReaderService.com or upon request from the Reader Service.

We make a portion of our mailing list available to reputable third parties that offer products we believe may interest you. If you prefer that we not exchange your name with third parties, or if you wish to clarify or modify your communication preferences, please visit us at www.ReaderService.com/consumerschoice or write to us at Reader Service Preference Service, P.O. Box 9062, Buffalo, NY 14269. Include your complete name and address.

Harlequin®

SPECIAL EDITION

Life, Love and Family

USA TODAY bestselling author

Marie Ferrarella

enchants readers in

ONCE UPON A MATCHMAKER

Micah Muldare's aunt is worried that her nephew is going to wind up alone in his old age…but this matchmaking mama has just the thing! When Micah finds himself accused of theft, defense lawyer Tracy Ryan agrees to help him as a favor to his aunt, but soon finds herself drawn to more than just his case. Will Micah open up his heart and realize Tracy is his match?

Available June 2012

Saddle up with Harlequin® series books this summer and find a cowboy for every mood!

Available wherever books are sold.

www.Harlequin.com

HSE65674

A grim discovery is about to change everything for Detective Layne Sullivan—including how she interacts with her boss!

Read on for an exciting excerpt of the upcoming book UNRAVELING THE PAST by Beth Andrews....

SOMETHING WAS UP—otherwise why would Chief Ross Taylor summon her back out? As Detective Layne Sullivan walked over, she grudgingly admitted he was doing well. But that didn't change the fact that the Chief position should have been hers.

Taylor turned as she approached. "Detective Sullivan, we have a situation."

"What's the problem?"

He aimed his flashlight at the ground. The beam illuminated a dirt-encrusted skull.

"Definitely a problem." And not something she'd expected. Not here. "How'd you see it?"

"Jess stumbled upon it looking for her phone."

Layne looked to where his niece huddled on a log. "I'll contact the forensics lab."

"Already have a team on the way. I've also called in units to search for the rest of the remains."

So he'd started the ball rolling. Then, she'd assume command while he took Jess home. "I have this under control."

Though it was late, he was clean shaven and neat, his flat stomach a testament to his refusal to indulge in doughnuts. His dark blond hair was clipped at the sides, the top long enough to curl.

The female part of Layne admitted he was attractive.

The cop in her resented the hell out of him for it.

"You get a lot of missing-persons cases here?" he asked.

"People don't go missing from Mystic Point." Although plenty of them left. "But we have our share of crime."

"I'll take the lead on this one."

Bad enough he'd come to *her* town and taken the position she was meant to have, now he wanted to mess with *how* she did her job? "Why? I'm the only detective on third shift and your second in command."

"Careful, Detective, or you might overstep."

But she'd never played it safe.

"I don't think it's overstepping to clear the air. You have something against me?"

"I assign cases based on experience and expertise. You don't have to like how I do that, but if you need to question every decision, perhaps you'd be happier somewhere else."

"Are you threatening my job?"

He moved so close she could feel the warmth from his body. "I'm not threatening anything." His breath caressed her cheek. "I'm giving you the choice of what happens next."

What will Layne choose? Find out in
UNRAVELING THE PAST by Beth Andrews,
available June 2012 from Harlequin® Superromance®.

And be sure to look for the other two books
in Beth's THE TRUTH ABOUT THE SULLIVANS series
available in August and October 2012.

Harlequin® Romance

A touching new duet from fan-favorite author

SUSAN MEIER

First Time DADS!

When millionaire CEO Max Montgomery spots
Kate Hunter-Montgomery—the wife he's never forgotten—
back in town with a daughter who looks just like him, he's
determined to win her back. But can this savvy business tycoon
convince Kate to trust him a second time with her heart?

Find out this June in

THE TYCOON'S SECRET DAUGHTER

And look for book 2 coming this August!

NANNY FOR THE MILLIONAIRE'S TWINS

Saddle up with Harlequin® series books this summer
and find a cowboy for every mood!

celebrating 15 YEARS *Love Inspired*

Get swept away with author

Carolyne Aarsen

Saving lives is what E.R. nurse Shannon Deacon excels at.
It also distracts her from painful romantic memories and
the fact that her ex-fiancé's brother, Dr. Ben Brouwer, just
moved in next door. She doesn't want anything to do with
him, but Ben is also hurting from a failed marriage…and
two determined matchmakers think Ben and Shannon can
help each other heal. Will they take a second chance at love?

Healing the Doctor's Heart

Home to
Hartley Creek

Available June 2012 wherever books are sold.